D1524233

THE BAD MAN

G. Warlock Vance

ELEMENT 118 BOOKS

THE BAD MAN is a work of fiction. The names of all characters, locales, and events depicted are the creative inventions of the writer. No part of this work is to be construed as REAL in any sense, nor does it feature or seek to mimic any person or persons living or dead. Any resemblance to "reality" is purely a coincidence.

ELEMENT 118 BOOKS
Asheboro, North Carolina
United States of America

Copyright © 2015 by G. Warlock Vance
ISBN: 978-0-9964793-0-1

All rights reserved. No part of this book may be used or reproduced in any manner without written permission, except in the case of brief quotations embodied in critical articles and reviews. For information address ELEMENT 118 BOOKS their website: https://element118books.wordpress.com/

First paperback edition: July 2015
First online edition: July 2015

Printed in the USA by IngramSpark.

DEDICATION

This book is dedicated to my excellent team of first readers, all of whom are "big guns" in my book. Without their combined keen eyes, and "beautiful minds," this novel would not have been possible.

Also, a big note of thanks to ELEMENT 118 BOOKS for making *The Bad Man* one of the first novels in a line of incredible fiction to come.

Prologue: *Certain conclusions*

I withdrew the automatic and stared at it for a long time. There were several bright spots of silver worn through the blued metal surface, marks that veteran soldiers sometimes referred to as "badges." My .45 had certainly come by these honestly, in and out of its shoulder holster a thousand times and more, as it performed what it was designed to do. I held it tightly in my right hand, turned the barrel this way and that, its gleaming lines almost hypnotic the way they caught the light from the street lamp near the car. I pulled back the slide to engage a round then lifted the weapon to my temple.

The muzzle felt cold against my skin, and I smelled the oil I'd rubbed on while cleaning it the night before. My thumb moved up, as if of its own volition, and cocked the hammer. The CLICK was loud in the close confines of the sedan, but I was not startled. In fact, I felt ambivalence, nothing more; not even relief that this would soon be over. I was empty, played out, done to death with all the whys and wherefores.

But I'd never shirked on an assignment, and I had no intention of doing so now. Papa Theo had given me a job and, although it meant damning myself to hell, I understood that I had no other choice. I would complete the task, or die trying.

After a couple of minutes, the piece began to feel heavy, like it had suddenly taken on the weight of my bones, blood, and sinews, not to mention the added gravity of my troubled soul. The nuns in school taught us that God forgives all transgressions so long as the sinner earnestly repents—from the heart, and with the utmost sincerity. I'd whispered more Our Fathers and Hail Marys than most priests, each time sensing at least some modicum of absolution for the foul deeds I'd committed. I'd killed for my country, and had returned home to find a job that required much the same: someone else in charge saying "Aim, and fire," a trigger for hire either way.

I laughed to myself as I considered how very little any of this mattered. Few people care whether men like me live or die. But that fact had no bearing on what I'd been asked to do. I removed the gun from the side of my head, reset the hammer, and slid it back into the holster. God might turn the blind eye to me gunning down thugs who made their living on the suffering of others, and, as an enforcer in that shadowed realm, He might even laugh to Himself if I decided to eat my own bullet. I was, after all, one of the elements that made the machinery of that world run smoothly—one of those who helped grease the wheels, albeit with blood instead of oil. But after ten years of dealing out death, I came to realize that the Boss upstairs might have a limit to His level of understanding and patience. If so, how many was *too many*? And what might happen when I finally reached that tipping point?

I considered the very real possibility that I'd already surpassed that magic number—the one at which forgiveness was no longer an option—but the vast majority of those I'd killed had truly deserved to die. They were cheaters, con men, and brutal individuals without the capacity to acknowledge the pain they foisted onto others. In this way, I justified to myself why I did what I did. Of course none of that amounted to a tinker's damn compared to what I was about to do: to shoot someone for whom I had the greatest respect, someone I cared about like a brother— Cain and Abel all over again. How could God forgive a thing like that?

And even if *He* could, I doubted I'd ever forgive myself.

After all, Samuel Sloane was my partner, and the closest thing I had to a friend. I'd been tasked with "putting him down"—the way the boss had put it (my earthly one that is)—as if Sammy were nothing more than a rabid dog. Perhaps that's the manner in which Papa Theo saw him; it wasn't for me to say. My concern was that I wanted out, and this was the only way it was going to happen. One last job and I'd be done for good with the business of bullets, and blood, and retribution.

1 – *Before the End*

Samuel Sloane and I sat in a black OldsMobile, waiting for Richard O'Neal to exit the building. Under the mercury vapor street lamps, the car's waxed finish shone the same dusky blue as our well-oiled weapons. The handguns were carefully balanced firearms; sighted in, loaded, ready. We'd been waiting in the back alley behind Flannagan's Pool Hall for about forty minutes and I only had smokes enough for twenty. I never seemed to think about cigarettes until I went out on a job. Some guys chewed gum, or sucked on Lifesavers. I knew one fellow who carried licorice whips. Whatever. Someone once explained how such things took away that nervous edge, but that was so much psychological bullshit. For me, smoking helped keep me sharp and alert. It also helped pass the time in a way that didn't feel like time passing—the act of raising the hand to mouth, drawing in the smoke, letting it out; it was Zen meditation with nicotine.

I cracked the window a smidge to let in some fresh air, but all I got for my trouble was the stink from the meat packing plant next door. The smell of blood and offal wafted in and Sam wrinkled his nose. I grinned. It always made me smile to see that big galoot make such a prissy face.

"What's the matter, Sammy? Surely you've smelled worse. Does the odor of blood offend your delicate sensibilities?"

"Hey Ben?" he asked.

"What's on your mind?"

To outsiders, it might have seemed that Samuel was ignoring me, but this was not the case, just his usual pattern of conversation. I'd ask a question, and he'd ask something totally unrelated. After a while, we'd eventually complete the exchange. I knew he'd get around to answering me, even if I was only trying to razz him. Sam was... well, truth to tell, he seemed a little slow. I found out later that Sammy was more akin to what some might call a *savant*— especially with firearms. His odd manner of speaking was creepy when I first began working with him, but I soon got used to it. I always figured Samuel Sloane and the rest of the world were about three minutes out of sync. Not his fault, not the world's, just the way it was.

"This O'Neal guy... Is he a *bad* man?"

"I guess so," I said. "He offed Vincenzo Carmalini's little brother; that shit for brains Jackie. He also killed Thomas, the boss's chauffer, in that firefight last week. The boss didn't give a damn about Jackie Carmalini, he was a stupid s.o.b. anyway, but he was pissed as hell about losing Tommy, who'd been his personal driver for going on twenty years."

"How did he die, Ben?"

I touched my pocket, instinctively reaching for the cigarettes I didn't have. I gripped the steering wheel tight enough to feel the rubber give, remembering the metallic smell that still lingered in my mind—a debt that would haunt me until it was repaid in kind.

I explained to Samuel how Tommy, who was never the most cautious of men, had been standing next to the car smoking a cigar while waiting for the boss to conduct business with another don. "I was in the passenger seat, but none of us saw O'Neal until it was too late. Papa Theo had climbed in back of the limo, Tommy had shut the door behind the boss and had just opened the driver's door when O'Neal leaped out of doorway and capped him."

It seemed unnecessary to mention how I thought the Irishman had been aiming for the boss and Tommy just happened to get in the way. I did describe how the bullets had thudded into his chest, forcing him back into the car. He had his hands pressed over half a dozen leaking wounds, but the look on his face was one of incomprehension—*How could this happen?*

How it had come to pass was obvious; a third grader understood the politics of turf warfare, and most certainly the notion that bad things often happened to good people. I might have been impressed that O'Neal had done the deed himself if he'd gunned down another badass from his own side of town, but not one of mine—especially not like this—right in my fucking face.

"And what did you do?"

"I pulled Tommy's body down into the footwell then took over the wheel. I'd been the one who had had to sit in his blood as I ground the gears and got us the hell out of there. I did so without anyone else suffering so much as a scratch, but that was largely due to the bullet proof glass," I said.

Unlike his driver, Papa Theo was the epitome of caution, which was why he'd survived as long as he had in such a competitive arena.

"At one point, I had the vehicle up to 80, but Tommy died before I could get him to a doctor. The boss sprung for a new suit to replace the one I'd ruined, but that hadn't made up for the stupidity of the act—O'Neal had placed me in a situation where I had another man's blood soaking through my shorts. I tell you Sammy, if Papa Theo hadn't ordered a hit on the dumb son of a bitch, I might have drilled him anyway—as a matter of principle."

"That why we're s'pose to whack O'Neal?"

I nodded, keeping my eyes on the door through which the man himself would soon emerge. Samuel looked at me and then out the window on his own side of the car. He stared for a long time, but I couldn't tell at what. He could have been counting the bricks in the wall for all I knew; it was impossible to fathom the depths of Samuel's mind. He might as easily be thinking of how to field strip his weapon in the least amount of time, or pondering how much he wanted a candy bar. He was especially fond of ones with nuts.

When Sam finally turned his head in my direction, he asked, "Then does that make me and you bad men too?"

"Does what?" I asked, not quite comprehending—my turn to be out of sync. "You mean does killing this fuck O'Neal make us bad men?"

"Is it right for us to kill people like we do?"

Lucky me—I always seemed to get the tough questions. Every time I worked with Samuel, he asked such things. None of the other guys would even talk to him. They didn't understand his odd way of processing information. If he said anything at all, which was rare when he worked with others, they would tell him to piss up a rope or shut his pie hole. Not me. I'd known Sam since I'd returned to the neighborhood, and to working for Papa Theo. We trusted one another, at least as much as men who used guns for a living could. Although it was impossible to be certain, I think Samuel enjoyed discussing the deep stuff with me because he knew I'd give him a straight answer, or at least try to do so.

"*Bad men*, huh? I don't know Sam… If you do what you're good at, does it make you a bad man, just because you kill people in the process? Look at that crazy German guy, Uncle Otto, with the deli a couple of blocks over from your momma's house—that schmuck used to be a *Scharfschüetze*—a sniper during WWII. He can't make a fucking gyro sandwich to save his life, but he killed a lot of G.I.s before the war ended. Herr Otto came over here soon after and has largely failed in the restaurant business, but, once upon a time, he was the shit with a Kar98K. Maybe he's still trying to do us Yanks in, only with crappy cooking instead."

I grinned. Sam remained mute.

"But you and I aren't so different," I said. "You can pop a round into a guy's skull from fifty yards. You're even better at shooting people then Uncle Otto was. My forte is strategy; I plot, I plan, and I consider all options before I make a single move. Those are the things we're good at—it's what we do—it's who we are. Does that make us bad men? I don't know. If so, how does one change what he or she is meant to be?"

Again, he hesitated, cogitating, letting the wheels in his slow mind grind away at the problem, milling it into some sort of powder intelligible only to him. Before Sammy could reply, I heard the screech of rusty hinges and looked up to see Richard O'Neal walk through the door. Ballsy Irish fuck didn't have a single man with him. It almost didn't seem fair, but then he hadn't been much of a sport when he'd plugged the boss's driver.

Some of the big time hoods, like this shamrock-loving piece of shit, gained reputations for cruelty, for guts, for bravado. O'Neal's shadow had grown large in the past couple of years as his men took over block after block of territory formerly controlled by Italian families for going on a hundred years. The man was a giant among his own sort, but Sam and I would soon reduce his stature.

We watched as O'Neal descended the steps from the back of the building.

"That's him, right?" Sam whispered.

I nodded and motioned for him to get out on his side the same time I did. I held out my hand and counted it off…

One.

Two.

Three.

We slid out of the Olds and were less than twenty feet away before O'Neal even realized the shit had hit the fan. I was closer and I think he might have even caught a glimpse of me raising my automatic, but before he could react he was dead. I heard Samuel's gun roar, from someplace behind me, and watched half of O'Neal's head explode onto the dirty pavement.

I stood there, aiming at the corpse, but there was no longer any danger. O'Neal's days of shooting back had ended. Samuel joined me, taking care not to step in the blood and fragments of brain.

"He didn't even hear us coming," said Sam.

"Not until it was too late. See what I mean about the element of surprise? Still, it never ceases to amaze me how you can be so light on your feet when you're built like a friggin' ox."

I nudged O'Neal's body over with the toe of my wingtip. "Damn!" I said. "You caught him in the ear as he was turning to look at us. A great shot, and *fast* too!"

Sam looked at the body then wrinkled his nose again as a rivulet of blood edged closer to his shoes.

"Blood smells like 'lectricity, doesn't it?" he asked. "Like a burnt up wire."

"I suppose it does," I said, "but it's no worse than the place next door."

"I don't like that smell."

I kicked the corpse back over on its face and laughed. "C'mon," I said, patting Sam on the back. "Let's go tell Papa Theo the deed is done."

2 – *Flipping the Bird*

The next time I worked with Sam was a couple of months later.   A jackass of a goomba named James Fincino had cracked wise to Papa Theo during a meeting. Everybody called the little turd "Jimmy the Finch," because of his last name, of course, but also for the fact that he tended to flap his arms around whenever he spoke. Fincino was a low level hood with lofty dreams. No way he'd ever live long enough to become a don, but he didn't know that. The Finch's uncle actually *was* somebody and, to his credit, tried his best to keep Jimmy reined in. His *zio* happened to be absent on that occasion—stuck in bed with flu. He'd sent Fincino to the session as a rep, hoping the guy might learn something. Jimmy the Finch sat quietly for half an hour then suddenly launched into a tirade, wheeling off absurd schemes, and razzing some of the dons about how they were "pussies" for thinking so small when they could easily "have it all!"

While only one of several princes, Papa Theo had officiated over this particular conclave. He'd sat there without saying a word, paying out the rope, allowing Fincino to hang himself. It was plain to anyone there that the little fuck was just showing off, trying to make a funny, maybe puff himself up into the bargain. But shit like that didn't go over well with the boss. After Jimmy left, Papa Theo told me to take Samuel and go "hunting fowl." He said that Sam could hold onto Jimmy while I busted his mouth and broke both of his arms.

"That way Jimmy can't talk at all," the boss had said. Hearing that made me want to laugh, yet Papa Theo hadn't smiled while saying it. Neither did I.

I collected Samuel at his mother's place and we took off in search of Fincino. It didn't take long to find him. The bastard had no sense of propriety, always hanging out in titty bars, acting like a big shot. His uncle had even given him a tavern of his own, but Jimmy was in a different joint that night, waving dough around like someone teasing a dog with a treat. And he was just that type of guy, one who sneered while watching a poor creature jump, and whine, and beg. The strippers all fawned over him in that eternal hope he'd let go of a few bucks, but he rarely did. Behind his back, they called Jimmy "the little miser bird." No one in that fine establishment, apart from Jimmy himself, cared if Samuel and I had a little "talk" with him. They were New Yorkers who never saw or heard anything—not their concern.

The club was called *B & Bs*. This supposedly stood for "Boobs and Brews." Most of the dancers and servers were fully nude, so this was one of those places where it was illegal to serve alcohol. One could, however, bring along his own supply and have it rationed out to him for a small fee. What a law. I always figured some genius in the family came up with that one. It had the feel of Mob kick-back written all over it.

Jimmy saw Sam and me enter, and his naturally pale complexion turned ghost white. We already knew that Fincino had a couple of guys waiting in a car outside, but when he motioned for the bartender to signal his men, I shook my head and the barman suddenly became engrossed in making certain the beer taps were functioning properly.

"C'mon, guys. What's this about?"

I heard that nervous tone ratcheting up in Jimmy's voice as he began to comprehend that this situation would not end well. I felt no joy with the task at hand, but I was not the least put out by it either. Like any machine, I felt nothing. Whatever empathic responses I'd once possessed had largely been burned out of me by things I'd seen, felt, and done—not only during the last ten years of working for the boss, but also while fighting in desert conflicts where I'd worn a uniform and flack vest instead of a leisure suit and tie. While Papa Theo had noticed my talent for self-preservation and put it to use (I'll get to that shortly), I suspect he'd detected another kind of vibe from me as well—one that was as placid as a frozen lake, but far more chilly. I still possessed the usual range of emotional affect for loved ones, but back then, I never allowed personal feelings to get in the way of doing my job. That came later, and when it did, I knew my time was done in this business.

Samuel had his manner of coping with violence—strike first, and with precision, thus getting it over with—efficient, clean, and cold-bloodedly accurate. We took Jimmy the Finch into an area where they kept the overstock of beer and went to work. The storeroom was well-insulated, which suited our purpose just fine. Jimmy had pulled the razzle-dazzle routine on us, trying to beg off, asking us to cut him some slack. He offered us girls, dope, and eventually a wad of bills with a couple of hundred pictures of my namesake. Sam and I ignored him.

Another minute passed and that fight or flight look flashed in Jimmy's eyes. Before he could take a swing at us, Sam grabbed his arms, twisting them behind his back in a full Nelson. He pushed Fincino down so he couldn't lift his legs enough to kick out at us, and Jimmy squawked like a chicken. He made quite a lot of noise until I threw a roundhouse punch that broke his jaw. One was enough. I hit him so hard I knocked the crowns off two of his teeth. After that, Jimmy the Finch could only offer a bubbling whimper as I snapped both of his elbows in the wrong direction.

Samuel let go of him and Jimmy went down like he was made out of lead. I picked up the cash he'd offered us and riffled the bills, seeing Franklin's stern, unchanging expression repeated a hundred times over—a cartoon that didn't move. I smacked his cheek with the money until he looked conscious enough to know what I was saying.

"Jimmy. Would you like for me to give this to Papa Theo as an apology for your running off at the mouth?" Jimmy's head lolled for a second and I smacked him again. He tried to raise an arm in an effort to defend himself, but the limb flopped around as if it been replaced with a rubber hose. I slapped the cash against Fincino's cheek hard enough to raise a welt, and saw a little fire come into his eyes—a look that said, "I'm going to get you for this," but I thought it lacked any serious conviction. In this instance alone had I underestimated the man. It would take some time for Jimmy to heal, but he would seek revenge, and soon.

I curled the hand holding the dough into a tight fist and would have let him have it again, but he waved one crazy arm up at me and finally nodded his head. *Yes, take the money.*

"Okay, Birdman. I'll give this to the boss and tell him how sorry you are for clowning when you should have had more sense."

As Sam and I turned to leave, Jimmy the Finch said something. I couldn't quite make it out. I assumed he was probably so out of it that he was babbling himself into unconsciousness. I ignored him and stepped into the john to wash the blood off my hands. When I finished, Samuel and I walked outside and got in the car.

I was, at first, surprised that Jimmy's men hadn't followed us in when we'd arrived, but then a particular reputation preceded Samuel and me everywhere we went. Most others perceived us not as run-of-the-mill strong arms, but as adjusters of attitudes—this, and probably much worse. They were right to do so. If we'd been called in, the mark undoubtedly deserved whatever he got—even if that individual happened to be James Aloysius Fincino.

We got in the car. I started the motor, but waited there, feeling something in the air between Sam and me. It felt like unfinished business. I asked him if he was hungry, knowing he liked a good burger with the works, but understanding even more that he enjoyed hanging out with me because I didn't kid him about being slow like some of the other guys. He gave me an absentminded nod, so I put the vehicle in gear and headed toward the diner.

"What are you in the mood for?" I asked. "Feel up to a cheeseburger and some fries?"

"I feel bad," he said.

"What's the matter?" I asked. "You sick?"

Sam ignored me, as usual, and asked "Did you hear what Jimmy said?"

"Nope," I answered. "Didn't catch it. Was it something good?"

"He said 'I hope he chokes on it.'"

"That's Jimmy," I said. "Too big a mouth, even when he can't open it."

A few more blocks ticked by before Samuel finally said "I'm not hungry," so I followed another route and took him home.

3 – *Feeling bad*

During the ride, Samuel asked me again if what we'd just done made us bad men. I remember shrugging my shoulders, as if I'd never really thought about it one way or the other, but the truth was that I'd been thinking about it quite a lot since we'd gunned O'Neal. I'd been dating a woman named Veronica for several years and, while patient, she confided that she wanted us to either get married and start a family, or quit pretending and go our separate ways. Letting go of V wasn't an option. Neither was raising a son or daughter and being unable to look them in the eye when they got old enough to ask what daddy did for a living.

"I feel like a bad man," he said. "Mama hates me."

I opened my mouth to say something reassuring, but we'd arrived at his mother's place. A few more seconds fell away while I tried to think and, too late, the moment had passed. Sam eased out of the car in that sinuous way he had. The guy looked like a moose that someone had trained to perform ballet. His mom opened the door to their little bungalow and, for a brief instant, I caught sight of her snow white hair piled atop her head in a bun, saw what seemed a sparkling clarity in her grey eyes—so different from Samuel's dark brown ones—an exacting kind of stare that pierced one to the quick. She glanced in the direction of my car as Sam slipped into the house. In that brief instant, I sensed absolute rage; Mrs. Sloane's unequivocal contempt for what her son was forced to do in order to help her make ends meet. Whether her anger was directed at the man who hired us, or at Jesus Christ himself, I hadn't the slightest clue. For just a second, I wondered if her hatred might include me as well, but then her gaze softened, she threw me a quick wave and closed the door. I glanced into the rearview mirror, saw my own eyes, as glacial gray as Sam's mom's, remembered something and laughed at my own stupidity. The woman's damned near blind. Of course she didn't need 20/20 vision to know me for what I was—yet another of Samuel's *bad men.*

I didn't see Samuel again for another three weeks.

4 – Bad mood, bad dudes

Samuel Sloane (who Papa Theo once affectionately called his "Slo-un") had the aforementioned talents of speed, accuracy, yet he also appeared to float on air with his fluid movements. His brain may have processed information differently, but his true gift was assisting in the correction of "situations." This talent provided him with a means to support himself and his mother. And, although Sam was one of the best hitmen on the planet, he also had the uncanny knack of asking questions that cut right to the heart of things.

Since he'd first mentioned that nutty bullshit about being a "bad man," his words had eaten away at me, making me question crap I'd never given a damn about in all the years I'd been doing this job—nearly a decade. I hadn't wanted to think about it, but after he'd brought it up, there it was, the elephant in the room. From the time I closed my eyes at night, to the time I closed them again next day. I just couldn't seem to let it go. The love of my life noticed, and did her best to distract me, but Veronica's kindnesses hadn't the power to blot out so much blood and sin.

Samuel Sloane, and his damned questions. Ah, well. He had his talents, and I had mine. I was the one who'd had real Army training, yet Sam was the true marksman between us, the one with the best eye, and the one who seemed to know everything there was about how a weapon would function after handling it for only a few minutes. He might have made a hell of an engineer, if someone had ever bothered to provide him with a proper education. But regardless of any 'What ifs?' Samuel did his job as deftly, and as silently, as a cat stalking mice.

In contrast to Sam's penchant for questions, I could do anything I was told with the cold, unbiased compulsion of a machine. I completed each assignment with a cunning resolve that was so ingrained it had become instinctive. He and I might have gone along doing what we did without a hitch for several more years, but then Samuel had started in with all of this "bad man" bullshit. As much as I hated to admit it, thinking about it had thrown me off my game. The constant sensation of his words scratching around in my mind was the same as having sand in my eyes.

I got to feeling rough around the edges. No, that's not right. The truth is that I felt *rattled*. I knew I'd need to get myself under control, and soon. Either that or I was going to screw something up. In this line of work, there is no such thing as multitasking, nor does one tend to get second chances. One keeps his mind on the job, and only that—period.

I tried to talk myself out of it—tried my best to spend more time with V and forget the ramifications of my particular career choice. I'd been doing what I do for a long time. What the fuck did it matter to me whether or not I was a "bad man?" We are what we are, I reasoned. Some search a lifetime to find out what they are good at, while others find their path early on. Either way, it's a kind of destiny, a thing that is meant to be, one that cannot be denied or cast aside.

Papa Theo once said "Benjamin, you are a methodical man with an eye for detail." That was me, alert to every aspect of my environment, taking it all in. I applied this sense of hyperawareness to formulating my plans, thus adding *strategy* to my skill set. I remember a lieutenant in my unit telling me that I had the sort of mind that was made for chess, but I never saw the point in playing a game where the pieces didn't stay dead. When Theo gave an order, I scouted the location, plotted the most efficient means of getting in and getting away without being seen. I located my target, killed him (there had been a few women, but it had been mostly men), then got my ass out of there. Sometimes I worked alone, but when I did partner up, I preferred doing so with Samuel.

After the night we whacked O'Neal, Sam and I didn't work together again for some time. I did not, however, remain idle. Papa Theo still had things for me to do. Upon rare occasions I ran guard duty for shipments of contraband, or provided back up muscle for situations where those materials changed hands. The boss seldom asked me to do such things, preferring to utilize my skills to his best advantage—the proper tool for the job—yet I didn't mind helping out wherever, and however, I might be useful.

I did everything I could think of to keep my mind off of Samuel Sloane and his fucking question, yet my usual level of quiet introspection became outright brooding. Veronica soon noticed how deeply this went and asked several times what it was that could affect me so. She suggested I take a few days off, but denial made me procrastinate. I was still at that stage where I hadn't quite admitted to myself how much Sam's dumbass question had gotten to me, how much his innocuous little remark had managed to penetrate my crocodile thick skin.

With my thoughts flopping around like rocks in a tumbler, one might expect I'd have had a brilliant gem of inspiration, but this was not the case. All that developed were cracks in my usually polished demeanor. It didn't take long for some of the men I worked with to also notice that I was "acting different." Some of them thought I was pissed off at someone—or maybe fucked up over a woman. I knew I had to figure this out, and fast, or word would get around and I'd lose whatever credibility I'd earned and their trust as well.

During my last outing with Joe D'Amico, who was one of Theo's better guys, he'd asked, "What's eatin' you, Benjamin? You got money troubles or sumpin'?"

I made up some bullshit about having had a cold and changed the subject. It hadn't been difficult. D'Amico was observant enough on the job—one had to be to survive long in this racket—but he loved nothing more than to talk about his own problems. He sure had enough of them: a wife with expensive tastes, a girl on the side willing to do all the things the missus wouldn't so long as Joe plied her with her favorite pills, six kids, all in private school, and a jones for gambling. The man was forever in to the local bookies. It seemed difficult to believe that, knowing what he did about how the family operated, he could be so stupid. The man just could not manage his finances, nor steer clear of his various vices, of which blackjack and five-card stud weren't even in the top ten. Still, D'Amico was okay in a tight spot. I didn't trust him the way I did Sammy, but I hadn't wanted to see him go out like he eventually did.

Papa Theo sent us to meet with the man who oversaw his waterfront traffic, a Pole named Stanislausky. "Ski," as we called him, claimed that a few of Jimmy Fincino's men had been asking dock workers a lot of questions about certain shipments. Ski had called Papa Theo straight away and the boss dispatched us to check it out. Theo had taken me aside to clue me about the "product" coming into the country. Usually, that term was reserved for drugs, which was probably why Jimmy the Finch had wanted in on it. The little son of a bitch fancied himself the number one connection for every fucking junkie in need of a fix in the five boroughs—and word on the street was that Jimmy was next in line to take over the whole shebang. This was not the God's honest, but then Fincino had no qualms about bending the truth when it suited him.

What the boss had referred to as "product" was actually a cargo of weapons he'd acquired in trade from some of our Russian counterparts. Talk about "bad men," these were extremely rough dudes in the *Bratva*. Papa Theo said that Joe and I were to receive three shipping containers full of Kalashnikovs, ammo, and a bevy of US made heavy armaments. This was stuff the Russian army had lifted from various G. I. Joes whom they had encountered during conflicts in Afghanistan and Kazakhstan. If any of Jimmy's men found out what was really going down, they'd take possession and sit on the shipment while Fincino called up one or more of the other family princes to try and collect a finder's fee for the information—his own little nibble out of a much larger pie. Papa Theo was only one branch of this extended hierarchy, thus there was a chance that Jimmy the Finch could potentially start a genuine shit storm since the boss was running this operation on the Q.T.

Papa Theo had explained that "This time the Finch needs more than a few feathers plucked." The boss gave me a sardonic wink and said, "If you happen to see him, you have my permission to permanently clip his wings."

Theo often expressed an ironical sense of humor, but his meaning was as clear as Russian vodka: Jimmy Fincino was a dead man, the Finch just didn't know it.

5 – *Combat zone*

Joe D'Amico and I met with our Russian connection, a guy built like a Kurganets tank, and secured the containers without a hitch. Joe hadn't been told about the freight, and he wasn't the curious type. He'd stood guard while I'd entered each unit to check out the goods. "*Ochen karasho*, no?" asked the Russian as he flipped the clasps on box after box of RPG launchers, AK-47s, anti-tank missiles, and several crates of what looked like fucking land mines. I guessed that meant "Good!" but I don't speak Russian. I tried to seem nonchalant, yet I was in awe—of him as he towered over me, but more so of the cargo. I hadn't seen such armaments since I left the combat zone. Unless the boss intended to turn a profit by flipping the weapons through the US black market, he must be preparing for all-out war. There was simply no other reason to have that kind of firepower.

Our business concluded, I made sure the containers were buttoned up, and arranged with Ski to have them unloaded into smaller delivery trucks, making it easier to transport the shipment to a manufacturing plant the boss maintained as a tax dodge. Joe and I wove our way through the maze of alleys and pier landings until we reached my car. Jimmy the Finch didn't put in an appearance, but his men were there.

That entire day and night had been just like every other one I'd recently experienced, with that nagging doubt continually pounding its way into my skull; a gift from my good friend, Samuel Sloane. One that kept on giving. This lapse in focus allowed a bad situation to get out of hand. Instead of concentrating on the assignment, my mind kept trying to wrap itself around all that "bad men" shit, not to mention Veronica asking me to marry her and have some kids. Without realizing it, I'd totally ignored the incessant pinging in my head—the one that normally announced *DANGER!* like an air raid klaxon.

Joe and I drove into a small parking area accessible from the freeway. Without a clue as to what I was doing, I stupidly drove smack into the middle of an ambush. We hadn't seen Fincino's men, but they must have pegged us as soon as we rolled in.

They opened up on our ride with a GE mini-gun. One minute we're slowing to curve around one side of the lot, the next, the Olds shuttered to a halt, sitting on rims. The engine gave a kind of belch then revved so hard it finally threw a rod. The cylinder blew out with such force that it made the hood of the car look like a tent.

Joe's side of the car took most of the damage, and him with it. Hundreds of bullets punched holes through the doors and fenders. Glass from the side windows sprayed into the cab, a waterfall of crushed ice that lacerated my forehead, my neck, and the backs of my hands. Joe's seat, and his body, blocked the rounds from getting through to the driver's side, each shot hitting his flesh like a mallet. He managed to cough out his wife's name, covering the front of his Armani suit with a lungful of blood. The poor fuck was dead before his body slumped over the dash.

I literally fell out of driver's door and rolled away as another burst of firepower ate the remaining bits of windshield and upper support beams. The top of the vehicle skewed to the left and was pushed off by yet another blast from the machine gun. The car's life's blood of oil, gas, and antifreeze gushed out the bottom, while smoke rose from the ruin that was all that remained of my Intrigue. The sooty cloud, and the wrecked heap itself, provided a modicum of cover as I crept away.

I elbow crawled to a set of dumpsters on the edge of the lot, slipped in a mess of fish guts and nearly cracked my skull on a metal latch used to open the stinking box. I cursed under my breath, took a quick peek to gauge the position of my assailants, then made a dash for a line of break wall near the shore. No one shouted "Hey! There he goes!" but then I was so jacked up on adrenalin that I probably wouldn't have heard them if they'd played a Souza march. I continued some distance down the shore then doubled back so I could come up behind them.

This seemed a reasonable approach, to move in at close range and cap every fucking one of them, or maybe it was only reasonable for a man with anger guiding his steps. During my return to the scene, my rational mind returned, allowing me to comprehend that not only were the odds against me—there being at least three, if not four guys in that car—I was severely outgunned. My .45 caliber 1911 automatic was no match against a GE mini-gun that could shoot well over 1,000 rounds per minute, not to mention whatever else they might be packing. I found good cover behind a dune with weeds growing out of it, but this left only one avenue of escape—the ocean.

An old sodium vapor lamp lit an area between their vehicle and what was left of the one I'd been in. This would mean that I could approach them with darkness behind me, but that once I was near enough to return fire, they too could draw a bead on me. It was the height of foolishness to rush them, but that whole thing about the element of surprise loomed large in my brain. It was a cinch they thought Joe and I were dead, so I couldn't figure out why they continued to sit there.

Unable to see my watch face in the dark, I began to count off the seconds under my breath. If they didn't leave by the time I got to a thousand I would move down into the lot and take out as many of them as I could before they cut me in half like they'd done to Joe and the Olds. I got to 874 when I saw the driver's door open and a tall son-of-a-bitch named Marone step out. He hitched up his trousers, pulled out a pack of smokes and started to light one when I heard someone from inside the vehicle say "That's right, fuckwad, blaze up and show the bastard where you are."

Marone flicked the flint of his Zippo, brought the flame to the tip of his cigarette and took a long draw. He chuckled, pointed out that they were practically spotlighted by the street lamp, called the other guys in the car "a bunch of pussies," and continued to enjoy his butt. Observing that their colleague remained on his feet, bearing no more holes than he'd had coming into the world, the rest of the doors opened and three other men got out. One of them looked directly toward my position, but soon swiveled his gaze, unaware of my presence. I didn't recognize the other three, but even in the dim lighting I could see what they were packing. Marone carried a Glock with a chrome slide, one had a revolver—probably a .38, one had a sawed-off shotgun, and then there was the asshole carrying the mini Gatling gun

One of them opened the truck and, for just an instant, three of them had their backs toward me. I probably could have dropped them then and there, but I didn't have

Sammy's eye for distance. My .45 held eight rounds, and I had an additional clip in my pocket. That wasn't many shots if a firefight broke out.

The one with the shotgun motioned for his companion with the mini to help him out. "Put that cannon away and learn some finesse, Paisan." Mini-Man hoisted the heavy artillery into the truck and I heard a THUNK as metal hit metal. "What the hell's wrong witchoo? You want *us* to die t'night as well?" He cuffed Mini-Man on the shoulder and bent over, momentarily disappearing into the dense shadow cast by the trunk lid. He reemerged hefting a five gallon gas can. "You git the udder one," he said and Mini-Man soon complied.

What they intended to do was now obvious—burn the car to mess with the evidence; make the hit look more generic. It wasn't likely that gas or kerosene would burn hot enough for their purposes, but if those cans contained jet fuel, they'd be in business—the lead bullets would quickly melt, as would every other damned thing, including any bodies. I sent up a fervent prayer that such was the case, as it would help *me* more than them. Mini-Man and the former shotgun wielder, now weaponless, staggered across the parking lot trailing Marone, with his Glock, and the other goon who held the revolver. The odds had drastically improved.

My instinct told me to make my way to their car, pop the trunk, and collect whatever additional weapons I might find there. The mini-gun was a waste of time. Arnold Schwarzenegger could apparently sling one around with abandon, but it was too damned heavy for me to carry and remain Mobile. Likewise, the sawed-off shotgun had such a limited range as to be practically worthless. The chance they might hear me opening the latch was greater than me finding another handgun. The next option was far more to my liking—to simply walk up behind them and put a bullet into each of their brains.

I waited until the men were an equal distance from the car as I was from my place behind the dune then I got to my feet and quietly descended through the scrub and sand. My rubber soled shoes were almost soundless on the smooth macadam. Rather than slinking low to the ground, I openly strode to their ride brazenly *hoping* one of them would turn and see me. None of them did. I glanced inside the vehicle just to make sure no one else remained. It was a nice Bentley that probably cost more than the four of them made in three years. Previously, my thoughts had been fuzzed over with my recent concerns, but I was now on full alert, my brain ticking away with possibilities, scenarios, and the probable odds of success or failure. In this instance, there was no possibility of failing and walking away; I would succeed, or I would die.

There was no one else in the car, so I aimed myself at Jimmy's men and quickened my pace until I was only a few yards behind them. Without breathing a word, I shot two holes in each gas can and waited for the quartet to react. They moved exactly as I'd expected. The guys with the gas stood in stunned silence while fuel gushed out onto their clothes. The stuff pooled around them, the heady vapor quickly spreading out so that even I could smell it from several yards away. Marone and the other man turned to look at their buddies, as if those with the cans had somehow caused this mishap. Although both of them were looking in my direction, their attention was on their comrades and the ruptured cans. They never saw me. I shot both of them a single time square in the forehead, insuring that neither had a chance to fire back.

I hadn't actually anticipated Mini-Man tossing aside his can and lunging for one of the weapons, but it didn't matter. One must maintain the ability to adjust for the unforeseen—to be the reed in the wind, bending, not breaking. He got a step and a half toward the revolver before I filled the back of his skull with two hollow points. I didn't check, but I'm certain both rounds blew away most of his ugly face.

This left Mr. Sawed-off. He stood with the nearly empty container, but didn't try to run. I saw the expression on his face morph from one of fear, to cunning, and then he opened his mouth—no doubt in an attempt to bargain. I said "Shut up," and popped him through the breastbone. He went down on his knees, tried to take in a breath then collapsed over the can before sliding off and onto his side.

I found the keys to the Bentley in Marone's front pocket, and snagged his Zippo. His half-smoked cigarette lay dangerously close to the spreading puddle so I snuffed it out with the toe of my shoe before dragging the lot of them into the quickly evaporating jet fuel, rolled them around as best I could without dousing myself with the stuff then flicked the wheel on the lighter and tossed it in amongst them. There was a loud WHUMP that seemed to suck all the air out of my lungs, and soon Jimmy's men were little more than lengthy pieces of charcoal briquette.

Marone's Bentley served as both transportation and hearse. I moved it alongside the destroyed Olds, removed anything that might have connected me to the car—including as many of my fingerprints as I could wipe down—and wrapped Joe's fingers around the wheel to make it look like he'd been driving. Next, I moved him to the backseat of the Bentley and drove the car straight to an undertaker employed by Papa Theo. The fellow was none too happy to be dragged out of bed at that hour, but after seeing the expression on my face, he clammed up and helped me get Joe onto a gurney and into his mortuary.

"Fix him up so that he's presentable for viewing. No need for his wife and kids to see him like this."

"Will do," he said.

By this point, I was covered in gas and blood. I was bone tired, and I smelled like an abattoir in hell. None of it mattered. Rather than heading home, I asked the undertaker if I could steal a couple of bricks from his garden. He shrugged and waved me on. He had more important matters to worry about, and so did I.

6 – *Hot wheels*

I dug up the bricks from around the base of some neatly manicured shrubs, tossed them onto the passenger's seat of my borrowed wheels, and opened the trunk to see what else I'd acquired. Along with the GE mini-gun were two full cartons of military grade ammo. The shotgun was still there, as well as a duffel bag and a small briefcase. I transferred the bag and case to the passenger's footwell and placed the mini-gun and ammo onto the back seat.

Although I look back now and see the strategy in my actions, I confess that I had no real plan when I got in the Bentley and drove to Jimmy's night club. I stopped by a Seven-Eleven on my way to pick up a couple of autoMobile oil filters, intending to use them as silencers for my automatic—a quiet way to take out Jimmy's lookouts. It turned out that I didn't need them. His men were not waiting outside or cruising the area. This was yet another of those traits by which Jimmy tried to demonstrate that he was the real deal, a total badass—he didn't need bodyguards 24/7, because everybody either loved or feared him.

With no solid idea of what I might find, I drove around the lot while my brain ticked off pertinent information, the data I needed to formulate my plan. No goons waiting outside, eleven cars in the lot out back, one parked off by itself in a side spot. Lots of noise inside, but the rest of the area was desolate, made up of shop fronts, some of which had been boarded up. Not another soul was out and about, not even punks hustling drugs, or pros shaking their asses trying to flag down a john. I pulled the Bentley around front and sat there contemplating my options. If someone would have knocked on the glass and asked "What are you going to do?" I would have probably said something like "Drive this fucking car down Jimmy's throat and watch him shit it out."

I watched neon lights flash in the windows and heard the loud music spilling out through the open door. If the lot full of vehicles was not enough, these other factors were all the proof I needed that a party was still in progress. Everybody knew that Jimmy paid off the neighborhood cops to stay away from his operation, but the local fuzz knew that he was such a dick, he would have ignored them even if they had tried to bust him. Always playing the part of big shot. That was Jimmy.

The Bentley sat within thirty feet of the front door. I considered hiding the GE mini-gun and ammo cans out back behind one of the cars then returning back to the front where I would jack up the rear end of the Bentley, place bricks on the accelerator, and send it careening into the open doorway. This would jam up the front entrance, forcing those inside to flee out the back where I'd be waiting. "That's one idea," I said to myself, but it seemed almost too logical. It fit perfectly with my usual way of doing things— cold, methodical—but this plan didn't match the fire in my belly. What I had in mind was meant to be payback for a multitude of Fincino's sins, and it had to be bold, and swift, and grandiose.

If I'd asked Papa Theo for his opinion, he would have sent in a couple of teams to carry out a bit of wetwork before leveling the place with whatever explosive materials happened to be nearest to hand. But the boss had already instructed me on what to do if I saw Jimmy the Finch. All I needed was to drive him out into the open so I could finish the job.

Or drive him further *in*.

I unloaded the mini-gun, and the cans of ammo, set it up about twenty yards from the entrance, made sure it was loaded and ready to go then removed the duffel bag and briefcase, placing them beside the weapon. I hadn't looked to see what was inside the bag or case, just assumed they were important since Jimmy's men had had them in the trunk. I climbed back into the Bentley, still planning to ram it into the front of the building, just not in the manner in which I'd originally conceived to do so. I started the car and pressed my foot all the way to the floor, the engine winding itself up higher and higher until it sounded like it would soon launch itself into the stratosphere.

"Fuck it!" I said, yanking the shifter into gear. The rear tires screeched like a tortured soul, calling Jimmy to hell, as they grabbed at the asphalt. For just an instant, the Bentley swerved to the right as it roared toward the building, but I yanked on the wheel correcting the trajectory—not the open door as that wasn't *grandiose*—the plate glass picture window was my target. *That* would make the proper

statement.

The front tires hit the lip of curb which ran around

the sidewalk in front of the building, and the whole car

bounced high enough so that the front end left the pavement.

The Bentley smashed through the window, the glass

disintegrating into bright shards—thousands of tiny knives

finding their mark in walls, ceiling, table tops, and

embedding themselves in human flesh as well. I saw all of

this, as if in slow motion, but didn't feel a thing until the

autoMobile ground to a stuttering halt amid the shattered

remains of the hardwood floor. The once gorgeous oak

planks had been plowed up into row after row of splintered

fangs. Likewise, most of the chairs and tables were mown

under by the broad front end of the once gorgeous machine.

Now that the car had stopped, the engine wound down to a

soft purr, as if waiting for someone to approach within range

that it might, once more, rage and destroy.

I kicked at the driver's door, but it was jammed.

Realizing that surprise and chaos would only buy me a few

more seconds, I drew my pistol and shot holes in the

windshield. I kicked out the useless remnants and crawled out across the dented hood.

The place was still filled with a fog of plaster dust, blown insulation, and other debris. Bits of electrical wiring torn free from the walls hung loosely from the ceiling, spitting out blue arcs of current. I stepped back outside onto the sidewalk through what remained of the picture window and nearly castrated myself on a shard of glass I hadn't noticed until it was nearly too late. Behind me, I heard the combined wailing of those who'd been maimed in the assault, and the beseeching cries of those soon to die. I had no way of knowing how many had been inside at that late hour. What I cared about was who might have come out of it unscathed and how many of those would fight back.

I didn't wait to see.

As I walked toward the mini-gun, I heard Jimmy's bird-thin falsetto cheeping out instructions, ordering his boys outside. I'm sure they all knew it was suicide to obey, yet here they came, one-by-one, staggering through what was left of the door and climbing over the Bentley through the twisted window frame. I stood my ground until no one else emerged from the building then I opened up on them with the electric canon. One or two of them snapped off a shot in my direction, but they were too disoriented. The closest slug caromed off the pavement about seven or eight feet to my left, and that was that. I blasted through one full belt of ammo in exactly three seconds, the bullets tearing off limbs, cleaving open chest cavities, and grinding to powder the bricks and mortar behind them.

I dropped the machine gun and returned to the ruined façade of Jimmy's club. Except for the Bentley's low hum, all else was quiet. I figured Fincino would have a weapon in each hand and six more piled up on a table beside him, but when I reentered the place, he was sitting at the bar with his back to me, a bottle of bourbon in front of him, a cracked rock glass in his hand. The bar itself was remarkably unscathed except for two or three holes punched into the cherry surface by stray rounds from the mini-gun.

Jimmy raised the glass, saluting me over his shoulder. "Here's to you, asshole! You killed my car, you fuckin' bastard. I can hardly wait to find out what Theo and the other princes do to your sorry butt."

"Whatever happens, you won't live to see it."

The destruction of his property, and the death of his best goons had obviously not registered, but that last bit finally did. He took a sip from the glass and craned his neck around to stare at me.

"You wouldn't d—"

Flame leapt from the barrel of my .45. His glass puffed to oblivion in a mist of liquor and gleaming fragments. Three of his slender fingers were shredded by the diamond sharp pieces, and the right side of his face was speckled with blood, as if some graffiti artist had gone rogue with a spray can and tagged his cheek and forehead.

Although Jimmy must have suspected that Papa Theo had sent someone to seek retribution for killing his guys, he hadn't taken the time to look at me—to truly *see* me. He did so now and as recognition dawned in his eyes, that part of his face which remained untouched by blood turned pale.

"How…?"

"You sent your best triggers to kill me and D'Amico. You can ask them what went wrong when you see them on the other side."

I'd finally gotten his attention, but he was too stunned to retort. I saw his jaw loosen, but whether in an attempt to reason with me, or get off one more jibe, I didn't care. My next bullet caught him just above the bridge of his nose. Suffice to say, Jimmy Fincino died far less painfully than he deserved to.

I collected my brass, walked outside to find the duffel bag and briefcase, picked them up, and returned to my own neighborhood by shank's mare. It was a long walk, but I was glad for the chance to clear my head. This had been one of the bloodiest encounters I'd ever experienced, and I knew, without doubt, that it was the beginning of the end as far as my career as a shooter was concerned.

It was nearly dawn when I knocked on the door to Papa Theo's. One of his guys looked at me in bewilderment and ushered me inside. "The fuck happen to you?" he asked.

"I need to see the boss—it's important."

7 – *Watch your back*

I expected two things to happen as a result of my rogue escapade: that Papa Theo would go ballistic and maybe shoot me himself; and that the other princes in the organization would demand my head on a pike.

Neither occurred.

Theo listened carefully as I explained—and I even confessed to being distracted just before the ambush, just not by what. After hearing me out, he rose from his desk, crossed to where I stood, and put his hand on my shoulder and gave it a hearty squeeze.

"You took Joe to our guy?"

"Yes, sir. I did."

"Good, Benjamin. That's very good. You did all right tonight. It's sad to lose Joe like that, but I'm happy as a pig in shit to be rid of Fincino and his crew."

I didn't say a word, simply nodded, waiting for the other shoe to drop, but it never did. Papa Theo told me to clean up in one of the bathrooms downstairs, and to stay the night in one of his many guest rooms. He wasn't asking. By the time I dried off and got back to my room, someone had turned down the coverlet and poured me a drink. I ignored the latter, but got into bed and was instantly asleep.

When I awoke, I found clean undergarments and a new suit hanging on the back of the door. A note pinned to the lapel said "Thank you, Benjamin. I'll take it from here."

I dressed quickly and was prepared to leave when I noticed the duffel bag and briefcase I'd taken from the trunk of the Bentley. Whoever had brought in the new threads must have moved them to the side of the room to keep me from tripping over them if I'd gotten up in the night. I'd been too tired to remember bringing them in, but now I was curious—not only about the contents, but why in hell I'd bothered with them in the first place. Fincino had been such a low life it was unlikely that anything belonging to him could mean much to me or to Papa Theo, but this was an assumption that proved exactly how limited my imagination could sometimes be.

The duffel bag was crammed with forty-eight bags of what looked like very pure methamphetamine. Each plastic pouch contained at least a pound of the stuff. I touched a piece to the tip of my tongue, the taste so bitter it was almost metallic. This meant that the lot was far better than anything Jimmy's connections could have created. To judge by the bag in which it had been transported, emblazoned with a red maple leaf on either side, it didn't take a rocket scientist to guess it had been brought over from Canada. Those Canucks had cool looking cash, some of the best rock and roll bands in the world, and they could certainly cook crystal.

My first thought was that this was too good to be true because someone would eventually need to be paid for the sale of their product. No funds would mean they'd soon come looking for Jimmy the Finch. Of course the joke was on me since I'd single-handedly taken out Fincino's entire operation. The owner of those drugs would think that Jimmy had been hit for the meth and the money it could bring in. Even at the lowest street prices, that duffel contained nearly two million bucks worth of junk. I seriously doubted if those expecting payment would take the loss without reprisals.

I'd decimated the Finch's crew, but I didn't stick around to see if anyone had survived. A single witness could easily place me at the scene. That would be enough to send a tsunami of trouble my way.

As if the meth wasn't problem enough, the briefcase held a sheaf of unregistered bearer bonds, to be paid to anyone who happened to hold them. Riffling through the mix, I saw that each one was for $10,000 dollars, and there must have been three or four hundred of them in the folder. Yet another dilemma because these had, in all likelihood, been placed into Jimmy the Finch's safe keeping by his uncle, intended perhaps as payment for the drugs in the satchel. Whatever it had been for, it was Mob money, which meant that I'd inadvertently fucked over my own clan by bringing it along.

The only thing for it was to talk things over with Theo so I could find a way to return the bag and case to their rightful owners. I stepped into the hall and asked to see the boss.

"He's busy."

"Until when?" I asked.

"I look like his secretary?"

The wise guy finally informed me that Papa Theo had meetings all day and wouldn't be available until the following evening. It seemed too long to wait in light of the situation, but it would have to do. Perhaps, in the meantime, I could figure out how to fix things on my own.

As I was leaving, Theo's man raised a hand. I stopped, thinking *Here it comes; he's going to ask about me killing Jimmy Finch, or what's in the bag and briefcase*. I don't know what the man saw on my face, or if he saw anything at all, but he gave me a curious look. Maybe he'd heard what had happened the night before and had done the math himself. I couldn't know for sure, nor did I bother asking.

"Theo says you should watch your back," was all he said.

"I used to be good at that," I said then stepped out into bright light of late morning.

"You going to walk all the way home?" he asked. I turned back and saw him grinning. He looked like someone had managed to dress a gorilla in a leisure suit from Joseph A. Banks. I put down the heavy bag, suddenly recalling that what was left of my Olds was either still rusting away in a parking lot by the East River, or most likely, sitting in the county impound lot.

"I guess so."

He didn't reply, simply tossed me a set of keys. I clicked a button on the electronic fob and saw lights flash on a ride in the boss's roundabout. A Lexus.

"This one of Theo's?" I asked.

"Yours now," he said then went back inside.

I unlocked the trunk, stowed the duffel and briefcase, and made my way to my apartment. I needed time to think, and to plan, but I had a nagging suspicion that I was out of options. One last job, I'd thought. If I could somehow manage to pull it off, I'd be free.

It wasn't so easy, but then of course anything worth doing rarely is.

I've been doing whatever Papa Theo asked since I was a little kid. Back then, I delivered packages on my bike to people in the neighborhood. I think I did that for six or seven years before one of the older boys at school told me what was inside those neatly wrapped boxes. By that age, I didn't give a rat's ass if someone wanted to stick smack in his arm or cram it up his ass, I didn't care that old Mr. Vinny received a monthly allotment of skin mags, or that his next door neighbor, a sexy widow of forty, named Mrs. Feagle, got a box filled with those tiny bottles of liquor like you can buy on an airplane. I liked the way they clinked together whenever I rode over a rough patch of pavement, or hopped the bicycle off the curb. It wasn't any of my business that the woman drank herself into a stupor by 3:00 p.m. every day, except Sunday. On Sundays, she went to confession and, presumably, told the priest all about the little bottles and what she'd done with them, but then maybe she had good reason to do so.

I did all of that until I was fourteen or fifteen, then I moved up to helping out in other ways, accompanying older guys on day trips, unloading trucks and freight trains, even helping to dump a couple of bodies here and there. I made enough money to keep myself in decent clothes and shoes, to buy all the books and comics I could get my hands on, and had plenty to spare to help my dad.

My pop was a good guy, yet even at an early age I could tell he didn't think like most of the adults I knew. He had a thing for numbers, even claimed to see them in his sleep. He was one of the best accountants in the city, but when mom died, he flipped out and started dreaming about the lottery. Dad just knew he could "win big" by taking advantage of his newly acquired insights. He got lucky a few times, but mostly he lost. After he blew through his savings, which honestly hadn't been much after my mother's medical bills, he drained my college fund then borrowed week after week, and month after month, until no one would take his marker.

People liked my dad and remembered how good he'd been at juggling figures, a little here and a little there, to save them a bundle come tax time. Most of them felt sorry for him, at least sorry that he'd gone soft in the head.

Even though they could no longer trust him to run a tab or place a wager, they made certain he was never hungry. They took care of him in that way that all families tend to take care of one of their own—black sheep or no.

I never counted the money I paid to square his debts, but I'm sure it ran into the thousands. Most people were more than decent about it, claiming the debt hadn't been as much as it really was, trying to let it slide because they all liked me and knew I worked for Papa Theo, but I insisted on giving them their due. It took a few years, but I eventually got around to paying the majority of them back for their kindness.

The only outstanding debt that I could never square was one to Nick "the Prick" Fibonacci; these idiots and their penchant for colorful names. Fibonacci was a kingpin from the other side of town whom my dad was into for a lot of green. I'd made a couple of overtures, asking to see him, but his boys would tell me he was "too busy" or give me some horseshit about him being "out of town." Eventually, I just showed up on his doorstep. A couple of his goons led me in and shook me down to see if I was packing then forcibly steered me toward a small office where I met "the Prick" himself.

Fibonacci was a little guy, not as tall as I was then, and he wore his hair greased up in a flip like Elvis Presley. I coughed to conceal a laugh, but he didn't notice because he was too busy running a little plastic comb through his oily locks.

"I hear you're goin' round town payin' off your father's tab; that right?"

I bobbed my head, *yes*.

"I find that commendable, yet at the same time, *stupid*," he said, aspirating the 't' in a slight lisp, creating a fine mist of spittle that spewed out onto his desk. "On the one hand, it's terrific you wantin' to help out your old man and all, but on the other, it's just too fuckin' dumb to spend your own hard-earned bread when it wadn't you that run up the debt in the first place; capiche?"

I remember doing a lot of nodding, agreeing with the man until it seemed proper for me to make my spiel about how my dad wasn't in his right mind, blah blah blah, but I don't recall ever getting to say much of anything until the meeting was nearly over. After building me up and tearing me down about twelve times too many, Fibonacci told me that if I really wanted to pay back what my dad owed I'd quit Papa Theo's organization and come to work for him.

"I can't do that," I remember telling him.

"No? And why not?"

"With all due respect, Mr. Fibonacci. I love my dad and all, but Papa Theo's the one who raised me. I came here today to pay back whatever my dad owes you, plus the vig, so we'd be square."

The guy looked at me, like he was seeing me for the first time, like it had finally dawned on him that I wasn't really the little boy he'd taken me to be, that I had already grown the cojones that would see me into adulthood. He cracked a grin and said, "Fair enough."

I recall allowing myself a small sigh of relief, but it was short lived. The tallest of Nick's men grabbed me from behind and forced my torso onto the top of the desk in front of me. Fibonacci snagged one of my arms and forced it over the edge. Out of the corner of my eye, I saw him remove a large knife from one of the desk drawers.

"Your dad owed me five large, little man, but the vig wasn't money, the vig was an arm and a leg. I say fuck the money, but I want the interest, *right now*!"

The crazy son of bitch was going to do it. He was going to cut me up unless I cried "uncle" and agreed to work for him, but I never uttered a peep. I squirmed my head around until I could get a better idea where both men were positioned, then I stomped my feet up and down until I landed a couple of solid blows to the tops of the tall fellow's Italian loafers. He let go, howling as he jumped away from my pistoning feet. I rolled off the desk just as Nick stabbed the knife into the blotter where my head had been.

The only other guy in the room reached for his pistol, but I pushed him back before he could get it free from his suit. There was a muffled BANG, but I didn't stick around to see what happened. I ran out of the room, found my way to the outer door, and fled as fast as I could. If memory serves, I grabbed a cab ride to Papa Theo's and spent the rest of the afternoon telling him and some of his men what had happened.

9 – *Nick, the pirates, and other bad men*

I guess that incident with Fibonacci was a kind of wakeup call—my transition from less-than-innocent youth to budding bad man. That was my first real scare, but then one sees a lot of crazy shit as an associate in the organization. I guess it adds spice to what would otherwise be a pretty dull life. How many people know how to bribe a cop? How about the best way to hide money in one's home so no one will find it? And what about that strange sensation one feels when aiming a gun at someone, and pulling the trigger? I confess there's no real thrill in knowing any of this. Most days, I'd just as soon forget.

Back to Nick Fibonacci; a lot of folks wondered what happened to him. Simply put, he died a very lonesome death. The guy I'd pushed when he'd gone for his rod died the next day from a self-inflicted gunshot wound. I don't remember his name, but the Prick had liked him enough to seek revenge. I was forced to lie low for a few weeks. Papa Theo tried to patch things up, but like most chumps in the family, Fibonacci was too damned proud to accept a truce.

He claimed his reputation was at risk it was ever revealed that a teenager had gotten the better of him.

Papa Theo was patient. He tried several times to make nice, yet to no avail. Eventually, things seemed to die down. I got to thinking the matter was forgotten until a couple of Fibonacci's men drove through the neighborhood one night and filled my home so full of holes it looked like a giant birdhouse. My dad took a slug to the leg, but was not seriously injured. I'd been on a run for the boss, thus out of the line of fire. Papa Theo never said boo about what had happened, but two days later, I learned that Nick the Prick and crew met with a most unfortunate "accident." He'd taken a pleasure cruise off the coast of Jamaica, chartering a yacht for himself and his men. Somehow, the craft was attacked by what Papa Theo called "pirates." Fibonacci's men didn't walk a plank, but they were fed to the sharks all the same. As a courtesy, Nick the Prick was set off on a tiny island with a day's supply of water and two bags of Lay's potato chips. While slim, he'd been given a chance. No one ever heard from him again, but then I never saw anyone shed a tear over his disappearance.

Nick Fibonacci. Yet another prime example of what it's like to be one of Sammy's "bad men." I mean, anyone nutty enough to torture a kid must be pretty warped. Bastards like Fibonacci give new meaning to the term. But of course, I'm calling things as I see them and maybe it's easy for me to justify killing because, with the exception of Jimmy Fincino (and one other that I will mention in due course), I can say "someone told me to do it."

Papa Theo had sent me on hundreds of hits, some with Sammy and some with other guys. A lot of my "assistants" ended up like Joe D'Amico, fertilizing cemetery plots. A cowboy would call that "luck of the draw," meaning firearms, not cards, but it's six of one, half-dozen of the other. Very few guys in this line of work reach retirement age. The fact that Samuel and I had lasted so long wasn't a record, but we were quite obviously blowing the curve.

Samuel Sloane... Every time I thought of Sammy, it took me back to this "bad men" thing. I thought about him so much I began dreaming of past hits—like the first guy I'd ever shot: Dr. William Kilgore.

Kilgore had been brought into the organization as Papa Theo's personal physician. He'd been highly recommended by other family members in Boston. He was sent here to replace some quack who'd earned himself a state sponsored vacation, caught by the local heat for writing his own scripts. Kilgore functioned well for the first few weeks, but lost his nerve after being called out to tend to wounded men whom another gang had gone after with an axe and a drill press. Soon after, Dr. Kilgore fucked up a prescription and nearly killed the boss. At the time, there was talk that the physician might have been a plant, working for a rival clan. The truth was that the poor fellow just wasn't cut out for this kind of action. Stick him in a small clinic treating colds and patching up scrapes, and he'd have functioned fine. Toss bullets, blood, and brains into the mix and some people get a little woozy—even a few doctors.

Papa Theo knew all of this better than I did, but with even the slightest chance this might have been a set-up, he was forced to make a statement that would send a clear message. Although I'd only newly returned to work, having done a short stint in the Army followed by four years of college, where I earned a Bachelor's in Business Administration, I was used to providing "muscle." Up to that point in my career, I hadn't engaged in the more nefarious activities for which I would become well-known. This soon changed.

Earlier, I mentioned how the boss had noticed my talent, but he had done so indirectly. After high school, Papa Theo kept at me to continue my education, but I hadn't a clue what I should study. I knew I needed a decent source of income, because I had to provide for my dad as well. Rather than allow someone else to decide for me, I wanted to figure out something on my own—I didn't want a handout, no matter how well-meaning.

Theo had been more than generous with me throughout my youth, but I didn't want to be an errand boy the rest of my life. I didn't know what sort of work to pursue, but I knew enough to see that I'd never reach escape velocity dragging my heels around that neighborhood.

For a few months after I turned 18, I didn't do much of anything—a few odd jobs here and there, and babysat the occasional mission for Papa Theo, but I mostly lived off a tiny nest egg I'd stashed away. During this brief interim, I read up on various careers trying to figure out what I wanted to do with my life. My mother had always wanted me to become a doctor; dad thought I'd make an excellent professor of Mathematics. Both seemed like pipe dreams. I convinced myself that I didn't possess the smarts for either field, but the truth was that I had no interest in those occupations. I did have brains enough to see that Papa Theo was correct about one thing—I needed to expand my horizons.

After that brief period as a kid when I'd naively delivered odds and ends for the boss without knowing what was inside the boxes, I'd become savvy to not only what I carried, but the enormous responsibility that came with the job. I earned a good buck for a minimal amount of work, yet a considerable amount of risk. Still, I understood that one received nothing for nothing. I knew that Theo would pay for any form of higher education I wished to attempt, but I didn't want that kind of debt hanging over my head. With all of that in mind, I gave very serious thought to the few options I had to choose from.

Before my cash ran out, I lighted on a solution that would kill two birds with one stone. I enlisted in the Army, where I could take a couple of years to decide on what I should study, and, by the time I opted out of extending my tour, I'd receive the G. I. Bill to help with the costs of college.

The Army taught me a good many things. I learned to keep my helmet on, and my ass down low, whenever the shit hit the fan. I learned how men can function as a unit, how it is almost always possible to look out for others while still looking after Number One. I learned these things, and all of the other seemingly inane knowledge that one has drilled into his brain during Basic Training. However well I accomplished the entry level stuff, I excelled in areas that are all but impossible to teach—the subtleties of war, such as, planning, recon, and effective use of resources. I never made it above Sergeant, but I was the one that the guys in my platoon looked to whenever the fun began.

This is not the place for those kind of "war stories." Suffice to say that I learned how to handle myself and a bevy of weaponry. I did what my country asked of me, but

73

after three years, I'd had enough. I was offered a bump in rank, and the prospect of officer training, but I rocked out. I returned home with my DD214 and took Uncle Sam up on his generous offer of financial assistance to further my education.

After thirty-odd months of sand rash, sunburn, and a mouthful of grit with every meal, college seemed a veritable cakewalk. I studied the general business curriculum, figuring I'd focus on something in particular when it came time to do my masters. Except I never quite got around to doing the MA. I completed my BS, then tried my luck at finding a job.

By the time I returned home, my father was teetering on the edge—here one day, gone the next. I did my best for him, stopping by to see him every now and again while working a string of meaningless management positions that promised much, yet were fast tracks to nowhere. I never gave up on any of these situations, but something always seemed to occur, nixing one job after another.

The first was with an uptown bank. I was a trainee, and well-liked by the rest of the staff because I caught on quickly, and not only to the demands of my own job, but how to help my coworkers. The manager was an easy going fellow, but he took me aside one day and said "Ben, any dullard with a high school diploma can add and subtract numbers. This job offers no challenges for a man with your skills and experience." I never found out for certain, but I think he might have caught wind of the identity of my past employer, a fact that would have made anyone nervous. He let me go, with two weeks bonus pay, a hearty pat on the back, and a wish for my "Great success."

The next job was with a company that did metal plating—one that seemed hinky from day one. I was forced out from this one after I caught the Production Manager macking on one of the office temps. She obviously wanted nothing to do with him, but was too scared to stand up for herself. When I'd intervened, he'd insisted that I mind my own business. I'd insisted right back that, as Personnel Assistant, such things were my business. He took a swing at me, and even came close to landing it, I'll give him that much. When it was my turn, I doubled him over with a blow to the solar plexus.

I got six month's pay, in cash, as severance from the head honcho, with the agreement that I wouldn't "consider legal action." I gave the money to the temp because the assholes sacked her too.

The last place where I worked manufactured some sort of widgets used in cellular phones. My title was Ombudsman of Public Relations. After a few weeks, most of the employees gravitated to me whenever they needed to ask questions or sought assistance with any difficulties. After seeing me in action, and perhaps realizing that his staff no longer gave a damn about him, the CEO canned me. This was largely due to fear and jealousy. Salvador Dalí said that "the thermometer of success was merely the jealousy of the malcontents," but with this guy came the knowledge that I could easily do his job as well as my own. He probably realized that no one would miss him if he was replaced and that must have scared the shit out of him. Two months to the day I'd started, this man informed me that I "should resign." I informed him that he "should kiss my ass," which was, of course, just the excuse he needed to fire me.

I felt no great loss when these various *opportunities* dried up, but in the back of my mind I wondered what my father would think—if he'd feel ashamed of me. Strangely, I began to ask myself this same question about Papa Theo too, and with such questions on my mind, I stopped by the old neighborhood to check on my dad. I can recall that day with crystal clarity. He looked thinner than I remembered, but he was just as animated—and just as crazy—as he'd ever been. As I was getting into my car, one of Theo's men flagged me down, letting me know that the boss wanted to see me.

Unlike my dad, Papa Theo hadn't aged a day. This didn't surprise me as he'd looked much the same since I'd first met him when I was a kid.

"Benjamin Franklin; stai benissimo! What the hell happened to that scrawny kid that used to ride his bike around here from dusk to dawn?"

I shrugged, gave Theo the requisite grin he was fishing for.

"But seriously," he said, "you look great. First the Army, and then college… I'm proud of you, son."

I was touched by Theo's words, but I tried not to let it show. Although I was too independently minded to be a brownnoser, I didn't mind knowing that what I'd done with my life had made the old man happy. Without Papa Theo looking out for me throughout the years, I wouldn't have survived for long—not in that neighborhood.

He asked what I was doing for living, but I was certain he already knew.

"Looking for a new position," I explained. I told him about trying my hand in the world of business, how it hadn't gone quite as I'd planned.

"You know there's always a place for you in my organization." I started to shake my head, but he said "Hear me out." I listened while he explained about a small international shipping company that he happened to own, how he was the "silent partner" of the operation. Theo said he needed a manager to oversee the day-to-day stuff, maybe stop in once every week or so to check up on accounts, that sort of thing, but that once it was running smoothly, I'd probably be free for other activities.

"I'll level with you, Benjamin. Once you get the ship back on course, the rest will bore you to tears. But, it's a paycheck. And," he said, as if as an afterthought, "it's legit."

I'd been away for several years, but I hadn't forgotten what I'd learned. That the boss thought enough of me to offer me such a cream puff said a lot. But I never for a minute kidded myself because, even at this early stage, I knew there'd be more to it than balancing the books for one of his tax shelters.

"Sounds like something I could do," I said then took a small risk, "but I confess those 'other activities' you mentioned intrigue me more."

Papa Theo smiled, shook his head, laughed. "You know why I gave you a chance when you were little?" he asked. "Because you were smart, quick to catch on, and when you asked questions, you always asked the right ones."

"I hope that last one was as well."

"It was," he said. The smile remained on his face, but it didn't so much as budge the serious creases etched into the flesh around his dark brown eyes. Some men had crow's feet. Papa Theo had what looked like hatchet marks made by a dull blade.

His expression was serious, yet there was a brilliant glint ablaze deep in those sockets as he explained how the job was just a dodge—a way to show the IRS that I had a viable career, and a means of paying my bills with bankable income. He had several guys on the books that had never set foot in the place, so he really did need me to clean up the paperwork, and for someone to show up once in a while to convince lookee loos that the place was a straight business concern. That was the so-called "day job," but the main assignment would be to serve as point man for his more important deliveries. "Maybe you'll ride along with a couple of enforcers, from time-to-time, to act as additional muscle," he explained, "but nothing so heavy as to twist your panties." I asked if I'd need a weapon. Theo frowned, said it probably wouldn't be necessary. Those who truly needed a gun would have one; my presence on those kinds of runs would be seldom, if at all.

"You've got brains," he said, "and most of these Dagos can barely walk and chew gum at the same time." He was exaggerating, but not a lot. His men were the type you wanted working for you—loyal to a fault, and tough as steel whenever and wherever a fight broke out. But speak with them for five minutes and it was apparent that none of them were candidates for Mensa.

"I need you," he said, "to make certain the drops are jake, and that my boys know when trouble's in the wind."

"And why will they listen to me?" I asked, knowing from previous experience that such men didn't appreciate being told what to do by a newcomer—even if I had been around as a child.

"Trust me, Benjamin," he said, "they'll do as they're told."

So I functioned as both Plant Manager for Papa Theo's company, and as glorified guard whenever necessary. Neither job required special insight, but a couple of the deliveries had been dicey—someone shooting off his mouth to antagonize the other side, and sadly, this was just as often Theo's guys doing the talking as anyone else. Whenever a "situation" arose, I stepped in to squelch the beef with tough diplomacy—"Okay, gentlemen; we play nice, or we take our toys and go home."

The first few of these gigs were similar to runs I'd done as a teenager. We'd usually take two vehicles, the cars would stop, we'd all get out, spread ourselves around, stand tall, look tough, make the drop, or the exchange, or the dump if it was a disposal detail, and get the hell out of there. I don't know about the other guys, but I generally received a couple of hundred dollars in cash for each assignment. This might not sound like a lot of dough, but trust me, it didn't take long to add up. Soon enough, I had money in the bank from the shipping position, and a few grand in hundred dollar bills sitting around in my apartment, and little to spend it on.

Even so, I never took the money for granted. I always assumed the day would come when I'd either move on to a "real" job, or Papa Theo would retire and I'd be forced out by the next prince in the hierarchy.

Of course knowing such facts and acting upon them are entirely different aspects of the equation. The assignments were so frigging mundane I began to think of them as routine. This is just the sort of lazy, bullshit thinking that clouds one's better judgment and gets one hurt, or shot and killed.

I'd accompanied Theo's men on seven or eight such outings during the first few months after I'd returned. That summer had been sultry, with the kind of temperatures that drove human beings mad. The neighborhood was largely spared from this heat-induced insanity, but only because many of the local hotheads had gone on vacations to Tahoe, Aspen, the Caribbean, Cancun—wherever. They were out of sight, but at least they'd not been out of their minds.

But the neighborhood was only one place, and Theo's boys and I visited lots of others. During one of the last truly scorching days of that year—this was nearing the end of September—the boss set up an exchange between us and a gang comprised of our northern cousins; the Capras. This family branch controlled much of the upper area of New England, but as far as the other princes were concerned, they were welcome to it.

Bruno Capra had never deigned to attend the shindigs the boss hosted, nor those of the other controlling forces. Some said he was closely connected to the deepest roots of the Sicilian Mob. This sounded like a bogeyman story to me—something to give Capra street cred he'd never earned. With Bangor, Maine, as his center of operations, what else did a wop like Capra have to do apart from create a legend for himself? Bruno and Stephen King, living in the same old town, both inventing horror stories to scare the masses.

Papa Theo and Capra agreed on a meet halfway between their respective cities. Technically, this would have been Boston, but neither of them wished to involve the Salieri family. The latter would have demanded a "toll," of sorts, for conducting business on their turf. Instead, the exchange was to be made in a hellhole called Lowell, just outside of Beantown.

Capra's guys picked the location—a seldom used rest area a couple of clicks from the town limits. Our team arrived early, so I took a stroll up the small rise to check it out. The facilities, if one could call them that, were built atop a hill with steps on either side going all the way down to the lot. The buildings looked as if they'd been put in during the 1950s. The place was spotless, but it still reeked like an open sewer. The parking area looped around the hill in a kind of horseshoe, providing access of the place from both sides. I didn't like this and went back to say so to the man in charge.

Even the minor exertion of climbing up that short rise had me in a sweat. It was because of that miserable humidity. I'd thought the dry, oven-like heat of the Iraqi desert had been bad—all that burning sand as far as I could see—but this was worse. Most of that summer it had felt as if someone had covered the northeastern part of the world in a glass bubble and turned it into a sauna. Sweat stung my eyes, and the smell of the toilets did the same to my nose. The only creatures capable of singing hymns to such weather were the cicadas. I could hear their shrill racket coming from the woods that surrounded the hill. Otherwise, the air was so thick, so deadly still, it was tough to breathe.

Instead of returning via the steps, I made my way through a small copse of trees behind an outbuilding that housed the snack machines. The woods held the promise of shade at least a couple of degrees cooler—a place to rest my skull from that pounding sunlight.

More than anything else I did that day, entering those trees saved my life. I had nearly cleared the woods when I saw two vehicles exit the road and make their way toward our cars. One of them continued on around the bend, but the other slowed and pulled into the slot next to our rides. Three of Capra's men got out, nodded to Theo's guys, and motioned for everyone to meet behind the two cars.

I stepped down onto the paved surface of the parking lot and felt the asphalt give a little, my heels digging into the melting blacktop. I was no more than fifty feet from where everyone stood. Both cars had their trunk lids raised, and every last one of them stared at whatever contraband was supposed to change hands—none of the boss's guys keeping their eyes peeled like they should have been. I couldn't believe that Theo's shooters would fall for such a ruse, but that heat made it next to impossible for most people to think clearly. From my vantage point, I saw what the others could not—a squad of four goons marching over the peak of the hill, each one packing some serious hardware. The guy in the lead had what looked like an old M1 carbine; another carried an Uzi, while two more held large caliber automatics.

I had just enough time to shout "Up the hill!" before bullets began to fly and men started falling down dead.

Pandemonium ensued, with Theo's men running this way and that trying to put distance and something solid between themselves and their attackers. To his credit, Santo Marino, the boss's lead man on the assignment, slammed the trunk down on the head of one of Capra's guys, breaking the asshole's neck. Marino ducked down behind the Chevy Impala in which the other crew had arrived and took brief peeks around the back bumper long enough to squeeze shots at the death squad quickly approaching. Marino got off two more rounds before one of those other wise guys standing nearby shot him in the back.

I heard the KARANG of bullets ricocheting off pavement, the THUNK of others slamming into plastic, and metal, and flesh and bone, but I continued toward the melee, bent over, with an arm raised up over my eyes to cut down on the glare. One of the boss's other men was slumped beside our second car, bleeding, but still conscious. I was only a few yards from him when he saw me. I started waving my hands for him to stay where he was, but he either misunderstood or just couldn't take the sound of artillery whizzing around him. He stood up, stretched out his arms as if reaching toward me for help then a hot chunk of copper jacketed lead struck him in the neck. He went down, his head cocked at an angle for which it was never intended, blood pouring out of his mouth and ears. His body heaved up in a final spasm and the hand holding his gun let go. It skittered toward me across the hot macadam and I scooped it up and began firing.

The man with the M1 had positioned himself up range from the rest of his crew. He'd placed himself on the crest of the hill, where he could see the entire parking area, but he was out in the open. I shot him first then dropped the two closest to the vehicles. Within the next two seconds, I got off three more shots and finished the rest, taking them out in the most logical manner based on their relative proximity, and what sort of firepower they happened to be carrying.

Although this all went down in the space of a minute or two, don't misunderstand and think that Capra had sent carloads of fuck ups. All of them were experienced, and all but one of them had gotten off at least one more round in my direction. I'd heard two bullets whir by so closely that I could have sworn I felt the disturbance of the air from their wake, but a moving target is difficult to hit at the best of times and this was combat, plain and simple—a thing for which I'd been trained.

Two of Theo's men made it through that debacle, but both were injured in the fray. I instructed the one that had taken the least damage to drive into town and find a safe place where he could phone the boss and get us some help. I stayed behind to clean up the bodies, tossing Capra's men into their Impala, and dragging what remained of our team into the remaining sedan we'd brought along with us. I even tried using a few bottles of soda to swill the pooling blood off the pavement, but I couldn't do much about the shattered bits of glass, and the various fluids leaking out of the cars. Our Buick would still roll, but there were a lot of miles between Lowell and NYC—too many to cruise the interstate with a blasted windshield and fist-sized holes punched along the hood and driver's door.

I waited just over three hours before a flatbed truck with a winch arrived. Two people got out of the cab, a man in a sweat-stained Red Sox cap and a V neck t-shirt so white it practically glowed, and a young woman in worn out jeans and a flouncy blouse with the tails tied up high enough to reveal her near perfect abs and a jewel pierced through her navel. They asked if any other cars had pulled into the lot. I informed them that there had been three, but that none had stayed more than a few seconds after seeing the aftermath of the shootout. "Did they see you?" asked the woman. I shook my head. No one saw me.

They shrugged, said they'd just have to work faster, and within a few minutes, they had snagged our car, tossed a tarp over it, and hauled it and the bodies of Theo's men to someplace or other. I didn't ask where. At first I thought it odd that they left behind the other car, but I reasoned that since it was Capra's car and men, it wasn't their problem. It would soon be found and word would get around. Capra would end up with egg on his face, if he lived long enough to feel embarrassed by such a lame stunt. Papa Theo had the capacity to forgive, but I knew from experience that he would never do so with anyone who had attempted to dick him over.

I watched the flatbed disappear around that bend in the parking lot and shortly after, a limo pulled in, slowed, but did not park. The driver's window slid down; the fellow told me to "Get in." Once I arrived back in the city, I explained what had happened to one of the boss's upper echelon. That was the last time I accompanied Papa Theo's men as an "assistant." On the rare occasions when I was sent out on such assignments thereafter, I was the one in charge.

10 – *Think it over*

Papa Theo took the loss of his men in a bad way, one that did not bode well for those who were now on his shit list. After he heard what I had to say about the meet with Capra's men, how it had been fubar from square one, he asked how I'd have handled it. I mentioned that none of us were ready for what happened—little to no data about the drop site, and no reconnaissance once we'd arrived. This was, I confessed, not entirely the fault of the men. The previous runs had gone down without a hitch, so we were unprepared when the deal went tits up. I left out the part about the crazy heat. It was tough to imagine such a thing in the relatively chilly climes of the boss's air-conditioned office.

"How long did it take?" the boss asked.

At first I was confused by the question. "You mean the event itself—start to finish?"

"No, son. For you to take down those men."

I closed my eyes, remembering every step, every shot, every breath. "From the time I picked up the weapon, maybe five or six seconds."

"So, what do you suggest for future situations of this nature?"

I raised an eyebrow, but said nothing. I got the feeling the question was rhetorical, that Papa Theo had something more to say. Theo knew his business. He didn't need me to tell him how to fix it. The boss never squandered his resources, and like it or not, I had suddenly become an ace in his deck.

"Your newfound abilities should be utilized accordingly," he said. I waited, not certain what he was getting at, but pretty sure I didn't really want to hear the rest. Theo offered me a handsome salary increase simply to continue doing what I'd done to Capra's men—except I wouldn't exactly meet people and kill them, I'd hunt them down then do them in.

I balked—how could I not? As a soldier, I'd done much the same thing as Papa Theo was asking of me, but that had been a different world. Dispatching one's enemies on the battlefield brought with it a sense of honor—each side knowingly participating. I expressed these facts as best I could. The boss asked, "Do you truly see a difference just because what you did was sanctioned by the U.S. government? Benjamin," he said, "I know you are a good Catholic, so I'm sure you comprehend that the destruction of life is murder, no matter how much patriotism you use to gloss it over."

I saw what he meant, and I agreed that he was right, but I just didn't know if I had the stones to function in such a mode—at least here, on the outside, out of uniform, and in what was essentially a role as contract killer in the private sector.

He asked me to think it over. Before I left his office, he said "One thing about being the enforcer... You have the freedom to choose when, where, and how, and you also know, deep down, that every cretin who ends up in your sights deserves everything he gets."

11 - *Choose*

It was around this time that my father's mental health plunged into a dim crevasse from which I was told he would never emerge. Unlike some dementia patients who occasionally "know" their spouses, children, and friends, my dad's mind fell off the map into a region of uncharted territory, so vast and so grim that he lost whatever meager portion remained of his former self. When left to his own devices, he sat at the kitchen table, a spoon in his left hand frozen in place, as if hovering over a bowl of Cheerios, and a ballpoint pen in his right, tapping out an endless string of dots and dashes—Morse code from a distant civilization beyond the comprehension of mortal men. He said nothing, only stared out the window, all day, all night. He no longer recognized me, nor anybody else, and he would only eat if someone stuck food or drink in his mouth.

I stayed with him for about a month, trying my best to bring him out of his stupor. The TV didn't interest him, but then it never really had. Nor did music of any kind cause so much as a twitch—not even to disrupt the discordant tapping of his writing instrument on the notepad.

The last thing I tried was reading to him. After leading him to the bedroom and tucking him in, I would sit in a chair next to the nightstand and read to my father from anthologies of westerns, detective stories, and science fiction, and chapter after chapter from novels by authors I thought he might enjoy: Joseph Conrad, Thomas Mann, Henry Miller, Louis L'Amour, Italo Calvino, Herman Melville, and others. It was no use. I soon realized that he wasn't hearing me, and that my choices in reading material were but a piss poor attempt to come to grips with my own dark heart.

I did the best I could, but it didn't take long for me to see that I was no match for my father's situation—he needed professional care, and by utilizing my particular skill set, I could afford to provide it. I checked out several places then arranged for his stay in the one that offered real medical attention, not just trained ass-wipers. On the day the van showed up to take my dad away, I visited Papa Theo and accepted his offer.

When I took the boss up on the career change, I actually had my father in mind. It wasn't the money issue, because pay from my straight job would have covered his needs, so long as I maintained my already frugal lifestyle. What finally got to me was how one of the doctors described my old man's condition: "I'm sorry to say, but he's no longer connected to this world." The MD was simply stating the obvious, yet he might as easily have been describing *me* as well. Although I hadn't had a real conversation with my dad since before I'd joined the Army, the simple fact that I would, most likely, never have another one made me feel as if I'd suddenly been cut adrift. Instead of falling headlong into the abyss, as he had done, gravity had let go around me and I would soon float off the planet into the frigid blackness of outer space. I would desiccate in that endless vacuum, and be torn to atoms by solar flares and gamma rays. And no matter how poetic the metaphor, there was no one left to give a damn.

The boss didn't seem surprised to see me. He briefly condoled with me about my father's condition. Theo acknowledged how much he missed him, and how seeing me reminded him of my dad. "You're your own man,

Benjamin, but goddamn if you don't have your old man's walk—purposeful, no nonsense."

Papa Theo said very little about what I was to do in my new position. Perhaps he figured I already knew how to handle myself, so it was a moot point to explain. His only comment on the matter was that "Some get a taste for such action," and that was it.

Once I commenced to kill people on a regular basis, it seemed the very thing I'd been put on this earth to do—that thing I'd been made for. I did so with as much skill and accuracy as I would any other job, yet I never developed a liking for it. *Never.*

On a day soon after I'd taken on my new role in Theo's organization, he called me into his office, asked how I was doing, and made small talk for a few minutes before pointing to several handguns spread out on his desk. I picked up a serviceable looking .45—an older model with a thinner grip.

"That's your piece for as long as you wish to keep it. It's not as flashy as the newer types most of the other boys use, but it's a fine weapon nonetheless."

I asked Papa Theo if the guns were from his personal stash and received the answer I expected, "Every one of them; tried and tested."

Having made my choice of firearm, Theo asked if I preferred a belt clip, or a shoulder holster. I took the holster.

"Ask someone for ammo on your way out. There's plenty, but if you are like me, you'll want to decide for yourself about the load and the slug."

I nodded, adding, "I'll find a quiet place where I can try several combinations, see what works best."

"Do that," he said, handing me the address of a certain physician in his employ, "then shoot this idiot when he returns home tonight."

12 – *God and the Devil*

I drove to Dr. Anton Kilgore's small home and scoped out the grounds before letting myself in lock pick gun, like those used by police. After making certain there were no other parties in the house, I checked out my lines of sight, my probable exits then sat down to wait.

After just over an hour of nervous anticipation (and yes, I was nervous despite my training and experience; this was, after all, the first time I'd been sent out to commit murder without government sanction), sweating rings into the armpits of my dress shirt, I began second guessing myself, wondering if I could actually shoot a man in cold blood. When Kilgore finally arrived and flipped on the light, he saw me in my black suit, perched in the gloom of his study like some buzzard looming over roadkill. He knew right away why I was there; it was perfectly visible in his expression. He hadn't run off at the mouth like most people do, erroneously believing that every situation can be amicably resolved in some logical fashion if one can reason with those he has offended. Kilgore just stood there with this sad look in his eyes. "I didn't know Theodore was diabetic," he said. "I damned near killed him."

Theodore. That was the first time I'd ever heard someone refer to the boss by that moniker.

Kilgore was scared, but after admitting his mistake, he clammed up—remaining two steps into the room, shaking like a leaf. I shot him, but I must've been shaking too because all I did was crease a new part into his snow white hair. Next I shot off his left ear. He continued to stand there, trembling, but glued in place. Apart from his knees knocking together in fear, his only other movement came when he cupped a hand to the side of his face as if to signify "Oh, my, what's all this?" I remember him looking into the palm of his hand, seeing it fill with his own pulsing blood then looking up at me, half of his face a red mask, his eyes all but bugging from their sockets in his terror. Seeing all that blood stippled on the beige wall behind him somehow steadied me, and allowed me to put an end to his suffering. I put a bullet in his forehead and his legs collapsed out from under him. His body fell hard onto the floorboards, his limbs twisting into unnatural angles. I took a step toward him, thinking to straighten him out as I'd done to more than a few G. I.s whom I'd been forced to leave behind, but then I stopped myself. I stared down at the doctor's body—now nothing but an empty husk.

"*Requiescat in pace.*" That was the first and last time I ever said such a thing. After that night, I never said another word to the dead. My job was to kill them; God and the Devil could do as they liked with them in the hereafter.

13 – *The question*

Damn. After a decade, there's been so many you'd think I'd lose count. But I never have. This is not because of some sick sense of pride in my work (other than this account, which I will probably burn after writing, I've never spoken of these jobs to a living soul, which was another reason the boss gave me the job—I never bragged about hits like some fools I could name); I carry these deaths with me like any good Catholic, wondering if God can ever absolve me of so many mortal sins. But since I didn't go in for gluttony, lust, sloth or any of the others, I guess mine are more like the same sin multiplied *ad infinitum.*

Anyway, after Sammy asked his question, I kept seeing those I'd killed, night after night as soon as I closed my eyes; a surreal parade of faces, eyes glazed over, yet aglow with accusatory indignation. From heinously bloody shootings, to the simple, almost painless suffocations—I saw them all. Each visage morphed one into the other.

There was a guy named Hall, who'd used his fists on a Mob girl, busting her up bad enough to put her in the hospital, thus ending her career as a pro. He'd refused to pay retribution—had, in fact, tried to run. When I caught up to him, I shot him in the sack and let him bleed out—a slow and painful way to die.

Another idiot, named Marcus, was a gunrunner from some Midwestern sinkhole who'd come up short on his orders one time too many—I bound his hands and feet with duct tape and stuck him inside a target on a firing range. This seemed a fitting end, and was one that Papa Theo, who appreciated irony, found apropos.

There was a slimy fuck named Jonathan Ramsey who'd run down a bunch of kids in another neighborhood close to ours. I learned that he'd done this for the simple joy of it, so my killing him seemed more than justified. That one had been a favor since the asshole was somehow connected to one of the other families. I'd intended to shoot him in the knees, the thighs—make him suffer the way the children had before they'd died from their injuries, but Sammy had been with me on that one and, before I knew it, BANG, the guy had a fist-sized hole in his chest. After that, I guess Ramsey didn't have the heart to pull anymore of his twisted shit.

So many deaths. Did they all deserve to die? Most of them had, but I'd never thought about it one way or the other before this. Now Sam's question had become a metronomic tick in my head. Why did he always foist such conundrums off on me? And why did it continue to eat away at me, like some dog worrying a bone? A part of it was my desire to have a real life with Veronica, but the situation was far more complex than that. I couldn't say for sure why that was, or why it mattered, but somehow, it did. It mattered so much that nothing could ever be the way it had been. Not for me.

14 – *The relativity of easy*

Sometimes the hits are hard. The one on Dr. Kilgore was particularly so, but I'd meant to write something about the easy ones as well. I mean, killing is killing. Whether or not it's messy, as in *gruesome*, or as in *complicated*, none of them have ever left me feeling clean. But occasionally circumstances simplify the equation—the style of the hit makes it a breeze to do the deed and get gone, but *easy* is a description relative only to the lessening of the challenge, not in how one copes with the aftermath of committing the act itself.

But just to demonstrate what I mean—here's an *easy* circumstance…

Shortly after Samuel and I killed O'Neal, but before I decided to quit the biz, the boss sent me out on a solo job. I was to whack some rich guy's wife. This was not the sort of gig I was generally used for, but the guy paying for the job was a banker who had helped launder family funds for many years, much in the way my dad had done before all those numbers crunched him. Mr. Fiduciary Finagler said he'd caught his wife stepping out on him, and worried she might flap her gums about how certain accounts had been managed. The fellow had supposedly told her to knock it off with the boyfriend, or take a hike. The next day, she sued for divorce. The banker knew he was looking to lose at least six-figures, and more to come with years of alimony. And after all that she'd still be banging the pool guy, or whomever the boy toy happened to be, so he assumed it'd be cheaper, and *safer* for all concerned, to make her disappear.

I hadn't known this story when I'd driven across town that night to do the job nor would I have cared. It wasn't any of my business. It did happen to be one of the easiest hits, ergo the reason I chose to include it here. What made it so was a strange series of coincidences, the kind of shit one simply cannot make up.

On the night in question, a low pressure system moved into the region. The rain didn't come down in buckets, it slammed into the city like a tidal wave. Between the heavy winds and the constant barrage of lightning, the power kept browning out. That fact alone made it a simple task for me to move about unobserved, but there was another factor that came into play—the lady I was sent to kill just happened to be wearing a pair of high heeled shoes. I generally spent days plotting the most effective strategy for each job, considering my various options, learning my mark's routine, and yet, I couldn't have planned for what occurred. Somehow, everything came together as if I had.

The situation played out like this—I found a place to park just around the block from the entrance to the apartment, which was a fairly posh joint the wife had let after the husband had kicked her out. I exited the car and held a folded newspaper over my head as I approached the entrance. The pages were a soggy glob by the time I reached the door of the place, but it had managed to deflect the worst of the rain and also blocked the doorman from seeing my face. He took in my decent threads, my neck tie, and assumed I lived there. I entered the building without incident. After that, it was a cinch to climb the couple of flights of stairs to her floor.

My initial plan had been to knock on the door, force my way inside, quiet the woman as quickly as possible. I had a silencer for my piece so as long as she didn't scream it would play out fine. I'd make it seem like a burglary gone wrong, a thing I'd done a time or two before, so I knew how it should look. Having noted her schedule, home from work by 6:00, a quick bite to eat in a local restaurant, and back to the apartment by 7:30, I hadn't counted on the woman not being there. When I knocked and got no answer I stood there in front of her door staring at those gleaming numerals—306—wondering what the hell I should do.

Entering her pad with the lock pick gun would have been the simplest thing, but I hadn't counted on needing it. Of course I was pissed at myself for not having thought any further ahead than this, but it was what it was—I had to deal with it and move on to Plan B, whatever that might be. If nothing else, my soldier's training had taught me to think on my feet.

I stepped across the hall to a place where anyone looking out of their various spy-holes would have a tough time seeing me, and prepared to still myself until I became just another shadow. The spot was near the stairs, but at such an angle that anyone coming up couldn't have noticed me until they'd neared the last riser.

I'd no more than slipped into the gloom, leaned up against the wall, and sopped a handful of rain off my forehead when I heard the clacking of shoes nearing the staircase. It was obviously a woman's step, quick, sharp, efficient. I stuck a wet hand into my coat and drew my sidearm; my lucky charm against further mishap. But at that moment, I didn't need luck, because that's when the chain of chance jumped the rails into the realm of the damned-near impossible.

The footfalls were close enough that in another ten seconds I would have been able to see the top of the person's head. Just then, there was a flash of lightning bright enough to make it look like daylight followed by an almost instantaneous crash of thunder. The lights went out. The clicking heels hesitated in their progress. I held my breath, gun aimed. The person soon decided to make a go for it and resumed the climb, there was another brilliant discharge, and, in that instant, I saw the gorgeous features of the banker's wife in a kind of halo-like glow. I thought, *There's no fucking way I can shoot her* because there was something about her face—a look in her eyes that seemed to indicate that she had every right to do whatever she damn well pleased. But in that brief, illuminating moment, she'd seen me too. She yelled "Oh, shit!" and slipped on the wet stairs.

I remember seeing her fade away as the light diminished, as if she'd somehow dissolved into the night. Then a screech of shoe leather—like nails on glass—and a *WHOOSH* as she disappeared backward into the black gulf of the stairwell.

Although the hall remained dark, a thought flashed white hot in my mind, of me reaching out to grab someone's hand and just missing as they fell. The image resolved itself into the sharp clarity one sometimes gets with memories from childhood. I'd been ten or eleven and big for my age. My favorite recess activity had been climbing on the monkey bars. A little girl named Jeanette Zupan was playing with me that day, both of us sitting on the top of the bars. We were goofing around, showing off for one another, when she decided to try hanging upside down. Before she could secure her legs, she lost her balance and fell just as quickly as the woman on the stairs.

In my mind's eye, I see myself making a grab for her, but only managing a fist full of air for my trouble. Jeanette landed badly and was taken to the hospital. The other kids had seen what she'd done—no one's fault but her own—yet I felt responsible. If I'd been just a little faster, I might have saved her. She'd broken her ankle and didn't return to school. I heard that the family moved away, so that was the last time I saw Jeanette. The look in her eyes was the same as that of the banker's wife—fearful, pleading, accusing—one that said "Save me!"

I heard someone humming a tune on one of the other floors below and the reverie faded back into the shadows. Some old man on the second floor was taking out his trash and heard the woman fall, but with the lights out, and all the commotion of trying to find flashlights and candles, it was over an hour before the ambulance arrived. She'd broken her neck on the way down. I left through the back entrance and no one ever knew I'd been there.

Like I said before, you see a lot of weird shit in this line of work, but easy as that hit had been, the hard part had been knowing that her fucking mook of a husband had lied.

She hadn't been the guilty party after all. I couldn't know that for sure, and yet, I'd seen it there in her expression just before she'd vanished from this world. That look had held all of the fear and pleading I've described, but along with these emotions, it had conveyed a message that would haunt me as badly as Sammy's connumdrum: "I'm not the one, you fool, he is."

15 – *It really was an accident*

The reporters eventually got the scoop from the old guy that found her. He claimed he'd heard her shout and fall, but the papers deleted the expletive accompanying her last words. Papa Theo called me into his office the next day and I was fully prepared to tell him he didn't owe me a thing. I hadn't done what I'd been sent to do. Before I could speak, a big grin spread across his face and, unsure what that was about, I kept my trap shut. He said "Benjamin, you're a man who respects others, who shows good judgment, and who has good taste. You're also a quiet kind of guy who likes to keep to himself. You know I love you for all of these reasons and more, but sometimes I think you're too damned smart."

I still said nothing, knowing the boss would either chew me out for fucking up or ask me to explain some particular point to satisfy his curiosity.

"So tell me," he began, "how'd you know this job would work out better if it looked like an accident?"

Looking Papa Theo straight in the eye, I said "It really *was* an accident."

"How do you mean?"

"The mark wasn't in her apartment when I arrived, so instead of taking a chance on jimmying the door I just waited in the hall."

Theo didn't give me a chance to explain the rest, just laughed and shook his head. "Too damned smart, kid. Good work."

He slid an envelope across the table crammed about an inch-thick with bills featuring my namesake. I thanked Papa Theo, but I didn't open it or even look at it. I stuffed it into my breast pocket and turned to leave. As my hand touched the door knob, he cleared his throat and I froze.

"You made our client a very happy man," he said. "Turns out he was still carrying life insurance on the woman. Since the cops already ruled out foul play, he's shitting in tall cotton, even after what he shelled out for the job. He threw a little extra dough our way, and I gave it to you."

"I appreciate it."

"Sure you do, but c'mere, I want to tell you something."

I walked back to his desk. Theo stood up and stepped around to meet me. He slung one of his ham hock arms around me, gave my shoulder a quick squeeze.

"Listen. I stuck something else in that envelope. A couple of plane tickets. Get yourself a girl, fly to Vegas, blow off some steam. Why not take the brainy gal from the library; she likes you more than a little, yeah?"

Yeah. She did. How Papa Theo knew about Veronica I couldn't imagine, but he knew damned near everything else in the world, so why should I feel surprised?

"I'll think about it."

He gave me another squeeze.

"You do more than *think*, goddammit! You get on that plane and you go; *capiche*?"

I looked down at the sunlight reflecting off my shoes, thought for a second about how clear everything seemed after a good, cleansing rain like that of the previous evening then did something I hadn't dared to do since I was a little kid. I put my arm around Theo and hugged him back.

"I'll send you a postcard," I said.

16 – *My tether*

My two-week vacation with my vivacious, yet "brainy," girlfriend, Veronica, gave us an opportunity we'd never had to spend more than the occasional evening or weekend together. With my irregular schedule, we'd only casually dated, and maintained our separate spaces, both physically and spiritually—not as yet comfortable with further commitments until… Oh, fuck it. That's all a load of bullshit, and I know it. It was me that couldn't handle a full-blown relationship, at least not when we'd first started dating. I was fine with the commitment part, but I never wanted what I did for a living to reflect badly on her—worst still, to endanger her.

Veronica knew I was the manager of a shipping outfit, but I hadn't told her the rest of it. I thought she deserved the truth, if we were ever going to have any kind of life together, and it didn't take much for me to figure out that I wanted to be with her—long term. She and I had met shortly after I'd sent my dad away. I'd wandered into the library looking for *The Lady in the Lake* by Raymond Chandler; I found her instead. She steered me in the direction of Walter Mosley—"Same vibe, different tribe" she'd said. Never one to mince words, I asked if she would care to join me for dinner. "Just like that?" she'd asked. I'd nodded, holding her gaze. She'd given me an appraising stare, seeming to consider what she was about to say. That was when I fell in love with her—that instant before she'd said "Yes." It was as much her expression as anything else. She'd had this look that said *You get one chance with a girl like me, buster. Mess it up, and I'm gone.*

With my father out of the picture, I wasn't prepared to deal with the consequences of losing V as well. She was the last thing tethering me to anything resembling humanity.

The trip to Las Vegas seemed the perfect time to tell her the truth, but I figured explaining to my girlfriend that, in addition to my regular line of work, I also killed people for profit could wait until just before we flew home. Sadly, the vacation was cut short; an emergency call from one of Theo's men. "Get your ass home, pronto," he said. So I never got around to letting V know exactly who I was, and how she sometimes was generous enough to share her bed with a very bad man.

We caught the first flight back to New York, but I missed out on all of the action. A turf war had erupted the week I'd left. By the time I landed at La Guardia there was nothing for me to do except stand next to Papa Theo at all of the funerals. The old son of a gun had managed to keep both Samuel and me out of the fray. He'd lost a lot of good men, but had managed to save the two of us. The boss had his reasons, but I'll get to all of that in time.

17 – *Bad as they come*

Of course this event only added to my deep affection and loyalty for Theo, but it also made me that much more protective of Sammy. Thereafter, we both unconsciously increased that regular pattern we had of watching out for one another.

Although Sam and I had never discussed it, a routine just sort of happened for us whenever we worked together. It began when we first met, so many years ago, and continued until things played out as they did, ending our partnership.

To an outsider, we probably looked like a planet and moon, the way we orbited around one another, covering blind spots, always moving. Somehow we managed to stay out of each other's line-of-fire, simultaneously making certain no one got the drop on us. This was one of those special working relationships comprised of a kind of telepathy, a thing I shared with Samuel alone.

We'd first met on the drop crews, shortly after I returned to the neighborhood, and to working for Papa Theo. Sam and I did those odds-and-ends runs—nothing to them really, both of us simply along for the ride with guys bringing in merchandise or selling off larger inventories. Our roles eventually changed when Papa Theo realized he could make shooters out of us. I never learned how the boss came to know about Sam's uncanny ability with firearms, but talk about your psychic abilities—Theo seemed to know everything about everything.

Once we'd been given our new positions within the organization, the work was always dangerous. I mean all hits involve some risk, but the ones Sam and I worked on were doozies, and whether or not Samuel realized it—I like to think he did—we were not only there to protect each other, but also to make certain that the jobs got done regardless, even if one of us died.

Some of the boss's hitters thought Sam and I led blessed lives. Others thought we were fucking spooks. I don't want to give you the impression we never got hurt. You'd be surprised to see how much fight can get into a man, even a scrawny bastard, when he knows you've come into his house to break his legs, or cut off a finger, or maybe wring his neck. Sammy and I got scratched, and punched, and bitten, and jabbed, and cut, and even singed on one occasion when a guy set us a trap by leaving the gas wide-open on his stove. We opened the door, hit the lights, and KA-BOOM! The blast blew both of us twenty feet through the air and scorched the hair off my arms and off Sammy's face. He had no eyebrows or lashes for over a month, until they eventually grew back. I could go into excruciating detail about what we did to that asshole, but does it really matter? A week later, we caught up with him, and he died. *Painfully.*

The point to all of this goes back to what I said before—that even when it's easy, it's never *easy*. I grant that picking chunks of ricocheted pavement and chips of glass out of my face are far superior to digging out a lead slug. Believe me, I know about the latter from personal experience—but that comes much later. I'd seen plenty of other men spurting from what those old mystery writers used to call "red points." Nothing heroic about it, and trust me when I say that there are very few men who can take a bullet and remain quiet about it.

The other thing I want to make clear is that while it might sound as if Samuel and I were close friends, we rarely saw one another, unless we were on an assignment. This fact is most important, especially as it relates to how much Sam's question began to work on my thoughts. If it had been any of the other guys I'd partnered with, I'd have thought he had a screw loose and forgotten about it, but Samuel Sloane's enduring sense of sincerity made that thing about us being "bad men" impossible to forget.

After we bumped off O'Neal I didn't run into Sam again for another month and even then it was only to nod at one another from across a room filled with Italian goombas, wise guys, and representatives from damned near every family up and down the east coast. This particular affair began when one of the boss's lieutenants called a meeting to talk about the threat presented by some new faction or other—probably a result of the conflict that cut short my trip out west. Such meetings were infrequent, occurring only three or four times a year, but if one believed the scuttlebutt around the neighborhood, this one was "Big!" On occasions like this, one was likely to see old capos scraping low to

Papa Theo, young turks spouting off in an effort to impress anyone who bothered to listen (almost no one did), and serious organizers who did their best to cook up better strategies to make a quick buck for the organization.

I think the dons used those get-togethers to network and to have a good time rather than to actually plan much of anything. There was always plenty of food and drink, and anything else one might ask for, including drugs, and women of various ages, thicknesses, colors, and persuasions. I usually found a cool spot against a wall, somewhere behind the boss, and stayed put until Theo decided he could gracefully bow out. Samuel would mingle, ignore the barrage of "dumb Dago" jokes flung his way, and eye the crowd like a human landmine sweeper just waiting to detect anyone that did not belong.

We saw one another there. I don't recall either of us saying anything. Seeing Sammy's sad sack, thousand-yard stare, brought his question to mind with renewed force and I spent the rest of the night examining every face while conducting my own private evaluation: *Is that one good, or bad?* In the end, I decided the place was lousy with "bad men."

It was, at that moment, that I finally came to terms with my position in the scheme of things—that no matter what I wanted to believe about myself and my reasons for killing, I too was as bad as they come.

18 – *The taste of fear*

The next time Samuel and I actually worked together was our last official outing as a team. I drove to the place he shared with his mom and he was waiting by the curb. This was another of his habits, unless it happened to be raining. I stopped the car, took it out of gear, and he hopped in. I asked how he was doing, how his mom was feeling, but, of course, it took a few minutes for him to get around to answering.

"Where we going tonight, Ben?" he asked.

I put the car into drive, stepped on the gas, and began telling him about the hit. I neglected to mention that I also needed to make an additional stop to take care of some unfinished business. The second part had nothing to do with Sammy, and it was probably stupid of me to take him along, yet I had no idea of how I could explain it to him.

Apart from the bad man bullshit, I'd been wrestling with another matter. Call it what you will, but it amounted to a guilt trip. I couldn't set things right, but I did have the power to add a little justice to the equation. Even though I couldn't tell him, I was certain that Samuel would have approved.

"Papa Theo warned me to be extra careful this time."

When Sam said that I came within an ace of slamming on the brakes and jamming my gun against his neck to ask what he *knew*, what the boss might have told him. I felt a prickly sensation as gooseflesh broke out on the backs of my arms and down the nape of my neck. Sweat beaded my upper lip. I licked it off, tasting my own fear.

I didn't stop. I took a deep breath and held it, concentrating on keeping the car in my own lane, while willing myself to calm the fuck down. I reminded myself that unless Papa Theo really *was* a mind reader (and I sometimes wondered if he might actually have such a gift), there was no way he could know what I planned to do. He'd probably figure out what I'd done soon after, but not before.

I took another breath and let it out.

"The boss is right, Sammy. You and I must be very careful with this hit. The guy's big. Bigger than you. I'm told he goes about 250 and can bench press a truck."

"I'm fine," he said.

"Damn tootin' – you're as fine as gunpowder. Don't let anyone tell you differently."

"Mama's feeling poorly," he acknowledged, finally coming around to my initial questions as he always did. "She's gonna die soon."

Mrs. Sloane hated how Papa Theo used her son, how the boss was always putting Samuel in harm's way, but she was pragmatic enough to understand that without the dough Sammy earned from pulling jobs, they'd have both ended up on welfare. And, like as not, Sam himself would have probably become a ward of the state, stuck in some nuthouse to rot until the end of his days. She saw this clearly enough, even through the rheumy film of her nearly blind eyes. The poor woman had taken a beating from life— preggers at sixteen, shot-gun wedding only to have her new husband killed in the war. Soon after, she got a job in a sweatshop dying cloth twelve hours a day, six days a week, only to win fate's ultimate booby prize by being involved in an accident at the mill that cost her her eyesight, and thus, any future prospects of making a decent income.

Mrs. S didn't like those who had anything to do with the Mob or the rackets, which amounted to about 99% of the neighborhood's population, so I was no exception. But, she tolerated me because she knew that I wasn't like the other assholes who sometimes partnered up with Sammy, that I not only showed him respect, I looked out for him.

One evening, a couple of years after I began doing hits, I arrived a few minutes early, catching Samuel on the jakes. She'd come to the door, let me in, asked after my dad, and if I wanted coffee. After the pleasantries, she'd cocked an ear toward the stairs, and realized she still had time to say something without Sam hearing. Mrs S. had stepped toward me until she was very close to my face, placed a withered hand on my left shoulder and drew me closer still. "You know I don't like you, Benjamin," she'd said, "but you're the only one that gives a damn about him." She'd given her head a quick wag in the direction of the stairs. "If something happens to Sammy I'm hiring *you* to put a bullet in Theodore's fat head. Just so you know."

The comment took me off guard, but I tried not to show it. "I'm sorry you feel that way, Mrs. Sloane, but I don't think I'm the right guy for the job. Papa Theo's been like a father to me since I was a boy."

She'd clucked her tongue and spat. "The son of a bitch should have done right by his own flesh and—" but Samuel had started down the stairs by then, and she hadn't time to finish.

All of that swam in my mind as I drove— memories, like scared fish, darting left and right. Samuel said something else, but I missed it and asked him to repeat it. He did so, word-for-word, a unique ability of his that always surprised me. He could repeat verbatim anything he'd said or heard, yet he couldn't answer a direct question until he'd had a chance to process it. "I said that she's gonna die soon, and then I will die as well."

I told him that was a load of horseshit. And on both counts. His mom had her problems, but that she was as strong as an ox (not exactly true, but the woman was far from feeble—the old gal certainly had her wits about her— no doubt about that). And as for this nonsense that *he* was going to die... "What kind of crap talk is that? Worst case scenario, your mom takes a powder—you think Papa Theo

would throw your ass to the wolves? Get a grip, my friend.
The boss values your skills a hell of a lot more than he does
mine."

Samuel nodded, but I couldn't be certain to *what* he
was agreeing.

The streets stretched out before us for many miles.
Sam remained silent. I kept waiting for him to bring up that
crazy shit about us being bad men, but he never did. We
arrived at the home of a Mr. Janson; *ex*-wrestler, *ex*-con, and
now *ex*communicated from the good graces of the family.
I'd planned for as many contingencies as I could think of:
wife answers the door, son or daughter sitting out on the
veranda (he supposedly had neither spouse, nor kids, but no
harm in being prepared), a neighbor happens to be visiting to
return a tool he borrowed, or maybe Janson has several
compatriots over for a couple of beers while they watch old
footage of him twisting someone into a half-nelson,
dropping an elbow punch on another wrestler's head, or
jumping off the ropes to body slam some poor schmuck into
submission. I hadn't exactly wanted to, but I even
considered that we might find the guy in the throes of

ecstasy giving it to the maid while the wife was out for a night at the opera, and so on, and so on. Planning for anything; covering all the angles. Get the picture?

Janson himself answered the door, said "I wondered how long it would take Theo to send his goons" and before he could take in another breath Sam and I let him have it. Janson had bright red carpet in his foyer, but one could still see the blood. Lots of it. Like the guy had fucking exploded. I pulled the door shut with a gloved hand and Samuel and I got back in the car.

The reports from our weapons had seemed loud, but most of the sound had been absorbed into the open doorway. I waited a moment to see if anyone stepped out for a quick look-see. No one did. We drove away as calmly and quietly as if we'd come calling and found no one at home. I hoped the next stop would go as smoothly as this one had, but I was afraid it would end up like one of those incidents I spoke of earlier—messy as in *complicated*.

Although Samuel had not asked his question, the bitch of it was that it still flashed in my brain like a strobe light. This thought aside, I confess I didn't feel like a bad man at that moment in time. I felt perfectly justified because I knew that, no matter what might follow, this thing I planned to do was the *right* thing to do.

We headed toward the suburbs. I made small talk, and Sammy gave me his oddly-timed responses. After twenty minutes of this, he must have gotten annoyed with me and finally asked "Who you gonna kill, Ben?" I gave him a quick glance. Shook my head and grinned then told him what had happened with that banker's wife, and what I intended to do about it.

19 – *Making it personal*

The next day I sat in my apartment brooding over what I'd done. It had been a stupid risk, and I'd broken the cardinal rule of my profession by allowing my emotions to get the better of me. Even when the matter was truly none of my concern (I mean, who was this banker's wife to me?), I'd made it personal. And, without intending to, I'd made things hot for the boss. Now the only thing to do was wait to see how deep of shit I was in.

I hadn't been able to sleep—no surprise, but I got up at the usual time, had a shave and shower, ate a bite of something, and had a cigarette to chase it. I tried to read a book, but it was no good. I kept anticipating the phone ringing. Papa Theo would be on the line asking what I thought I'd accomplished in offing the family's chief money launderer; maybe to inquire if, perhaps, I hadn't taken a header off the deep end.

I waited.

No ring.

I finally worked up the nerve to phone in for instructions. The guy on the other end sounded okay, totally nonchalant, and said "You got a couple of days comin' so get some sleep." This was just a bullshit way of letting me know I was off the hook for forty-eight hours unless absolutely needed. I should have felt relieved, but somehow my anxiety tuned up a notch. After circling the living room six or eight times and smoking almost as many butts, I realized I had to get the hell out of there and find out whatever I could—if word had reached anyone else on the street about the banker's death and what, if anything, would be done about it.

20 – *Cagliostro buys Hemingway*

To make things seem routine I headed over to my regular job, Papa Theo's shipping outfit: *Gloria Monday Transit*. I'd outfitted my office with a handsome desk of Brazilian heartwood, which looked almost purple in the light of the overhead fluorescents. I also had a chair that, while nine years old, still looked new because it had barely registered the impression of my ass. The door had a large pane of frosted glass with fancy, painted letters reading *Giuseppe Balsamo, Overseas Distribution Manager*. I had not been born a "Giuseppe," let alone a "Balsamo," but that's what it said on my driver's license and social security card, and it's the name I used each year when filling out my taxes. I doubted whether the IRS caught the joke since they generally limited their focus to tax fraud, and couldn't have cared less that I shared the same name as an eighteenth century Italian adventurer rumored to have been a master of the dark arts.

Each month GMT's payroll clerk left a check on my desk blotter and was also kind enough to flip over the calendar whenever appropriate. On paper, I earned a decent salary from *Gloria Monday Transit* and, since I lived within my means, I was able to sock away a good percentage of what I made there. After paying for my father's care, I invested a meager sum each month in the stock market, and dumped more into a retirement fund. This was how most of the serious talent in the organization got paid—through legitimate businesses functioning at a far-remove from the dons' various other endeavors. And, as one of Papa Theo's problem solvers, I was provided with occasional cash bonuses. A lot of the fellows called such funds *hazard pay*. For these windfalls, I used another network to funnel the bills into a couple of private bank accounts—one of which was not in this country.

And then there were the books. Veronica held an MA in Special Collection Curating, and had worked around books most of her adult life, so she clued me in on the fact that rare books were also a good investment. I added a few titles to my collection each month. Of the latter, I had well-organized shelves full. As an avid reader, I enjoyed having them; as a librarian, she enjoyed assisting me to build a private stash of quality titles that matched our combined interests. Out of respect for V, I'd alphabetized the lot by authors' last names, and she later separated them into fiction and non-fiction. She once said that "When we finally move in together, these books must be divided by genre as well." For those who ever wondered if librarians are anal retentive, the answer is—YES. Of course, this goes double for any hitman worth his salt. A match made in heaven, even if I hadn't much of chance of ending up there myself.

When I entered GMT that day, my "supervisor" gave me a hearty hi-ho, same as always, asked me how I thought the Yankees would do this season, if I thought they'd kick the Bo-Sox's collective asses for them, and yadda-yadda. If he knew anything about what I'd been up to the night before, he was better at hiding it than I gave him credit for. I sat in my office, made a couple of local calls just to be doing something, saw a message from a book dealer named Arnheim, and, in under an hour, I was in my car and cruising out of the industrial area and back into the city. I simply could not sit still with this sword of Damocles hanging over me.

I filled the rest of afternoon doing all of the boring shit I usually do during days off—visiting the bank (not the one where the guy I'd killed had worked), dropping off laundry, having lunch downtown, picking up groceries, my normal routine—business as usual. From what I could determine, no one had heard a thing. Later, I drove to see the book dealer and haggled with him over a signed copy of Ernest Hemingway's *Death in the Afternoon*. He eventually came down to a price that seemed justifiably sane for a guy who presumably worked as a glorified shipping clerk. Arnheim also showed me a first printing of *The Sun Also Rises*, my favorite of Hemingway's uneven output. He nonchalantly proclaimed that one a "bargain at twenty thousand."

Arnheim moved on to a letter from Mark Twain to one of his lesser known contemporaries, but I explained that I hadn't yet branched out into collecting ephemera. "You will, Mr. Cagliostro," he said. At least he saw the humor in my Italian nom de guerre.

Recalling my interest in modern first editions, I followed him to a shelf near the front of his shop, from whence he took down a pair of inscribed copies of books—one from Don DeLillo to Paul Auster, the other from Auster to DeLillo. Arnheim informed me that the practice of authors signing books to one another was not uncommon. It made sense in this case because DeLillo and Auster were good friends and both native New Yorkers. The price of those two copies was reasonable, so I took those as well.

Next, I saw a Shakespeare *First Folio*, which was obviously a forgery, but a very good one, and still quite pricey. After that, Arnheim showed me a numbered, yet somehow unbound copy of a book by D. H. Lawrence, of which the title escapes me. Most of these were out of my league as a collector of "modest means," but as the dealer likes to say, "One can always dream."

He wrapped my purchases in a thick brown paper, claiming that "Anyone who does it differently is *not* a professional!" I got back in the car and drove home where I tried my best to relax. But not even the prospect of reading from a signed copy of Hemingway could soothe my jangled nerves. Sleep was a long time coming that night, and the next one, and the next.

After a solid week spent anticipating plague, floods, and an invasion of locusts, I came to the determination that, regardless of the pet money launderer's position within the family, life somehow went on without him. Things eventually settled, as they always do. I got to thinking that maybe nobody had even missed the asshole banker, but soon enough, a different kind of shit storm began, bringing with it a flurry of woe, and the death of twenty-seven more people—most of them by my own hand.

21 – *Asshole banker*

I found out the creep's name before making it my business to take him out, but "Asshole banker" is how I remember him. And to think, I'd once aspired to become one myself. Ugh.

When I consider what I did to that bastard, and the many others to whom I'd been legitimately assigned, I sometimes marvel over the depths of depravity to which I was capable of sinking. The individuals I'd killed during my Army tour were one thing; insurgents bent of destroying a few of Uncle Sam's boys and their toys with landmines, Russian made ordinance, or a fucking vest filled with C-4; maybe even a division of the Taliban willing to duke it out man-to-man, with both sides giving it all we had. Whether or not one believes in the necessity of war is a matter of opinion, yet most would agree that what I did for the organization went beyond the pale. The thought of slipping into someone's private dwelling to murder them—that's a chilly bit of work. I did this very thing for many years, with a great deal of success, and with only a modicum of conscience, at least until Sammy asked his question.

This situation marks four more deaths for which I am accountable. That's certainly not a record, but I never took pride in tallying my kills. Putting a lead pill into the banker was yet another in a long list of things I'd hoped to, someday, forget. That's why I didn't go into details about my little off-the-books adventure, but what the hell, I've come this far, why balk now? The man's death was an *execution*, plain and simple. There was the asshole himself, a guy so fucking scared he couldn't speak without stuttering, and there was the other asshole—*me*. I strode into what remained of his life, as unrelenting as karma, the hand of Justice come to snuff out his miserable and pointless existence.

I regret the way I handled things, but I don't feel remorse for killing him. The prick lived in the Heights on a tree-lined street that looked a lot like the set of *It's a Wonderful Life*. With all the money he'd siphoned off the accounts of poor folks who did their banking with him, it probably had been "wonderful," maybe downright *amazing*, at least until I showed up to roll the end credits.

Mr. Asshole lived in a big Georgian number with a gaudy, iron rail fence running around the front yard. As if the house wasn't showy enough on its own, he'd painted the front door robin egg blue. I parked the car a few houses away and shut off the motor to wait. Samuel took out his piece in anticipation, placing it on his lap with the barrel pointed away from me like he always did. I told him to put it away. "You don't need to be involved in this, my friend."

We sat there for maybe half an hour, not saying anything, just staring at all those windows. Must have been fifteen or twenty of them. That part didn't make any difference to me. I'd search from room to room to locate him, if I had to. And if, by some miracle, he managed to elude me, I'd still find him. One way or another, the man was already as good as dead—he just didn't know it.

A car passed, yet didn't stop. I wanted to smoke, but I couldn't risk some Lookee Lou peering out the curtains and getting suspicious over a couple of guys sitting in a dark car at one in the morning. Such activity was *de rigor* back in our own neighborhood; not the case on this swanky street. After determining that no one seemed to be awake in the general vicinity, I got out of the car, quickly scanning the yards and fronts of houses nearby. I let my eyes adjust to the gloom, until I could be certain there was no movement on that side of the street. During those few seconds, I spied a small side gate and made my way toward it. There was no lock, so I unlatched it and went through. I took a single step toward the house when I suddenly felt something push against my thigh. There was a muffled "Woof!" and my heart lurched a beat as I saw a huge mutt, muscles bunched as if to pounce, jaws dripping saliva in ropey strings. I stared at it, unmoving; it stared squarely at my crotch, its breath puffing out in a foggy plume, waiting for me to do whatever I was going to do.

The beast looked like a strange crossbreeding between a Greyhound and a Bull Mastiff. It didn't make another sound, nor did it lunge; just the same, it didn't look like it intended on getting out of my way either. I moved back and felt my ass pinned against the cold steel bars of the closed gate. I wasn't going anywhere and the dog knew it. The gun was in my holster and it would have been a breeze to snag it and pop a cap in the pooch's skull, but I didn't want to do that for all kinds of reasons. Even with the silencer there would have been a POP and a muzzle flash, both of which might warn Asshole Banker of my intentions. More to the point, I was thinking of the dog. The brute hadn't done anything wrong—was, in fact, doing exactly what it was supposed to. It wasn't the animal's fault it had gotten fucked by fate. Just as human beings can't choose their parents, pets choose their masters. More's the pity.

I stuck my hand in my pocket and felt something solid. I thought at first it was a lead sap, but it wasn't heavy enough for that. I brought it out and saw the squished curl of a partially melted Payday bar, which I'd intended to give to Sammy. At the sound of the crinkling paper the dog's tail began to wag and it came over and stuck its nose up in my groin. "That's right," I said. "I'm Ben, the guy who's come to make you an orphan." I took the wrapper in between my teeth and tore it open then squeezed out a gooey portion. Fido licked at the melting caramel, sniffed a couple of times, and before I knew it, snarfed up the entire thing, paper and all. I barely got my hand out of the way. If I hadn't, the dog might have eaten that too.

After that, we were best pals. I held the animal's collar and turned the tag toward the street lamp. In the brief flare of reflected light, I read BRUTUS, and barely suppressed a laugh, thinking *I have come to bury Caesar.* He allowed me to pet him and, looking into his comically smushed face, I thought he seemed dopey, like he was long overdue on sleep. He rolled onto his back so I could rub his belly then yawned.

"Late night, huh? I know how you feel," I whispered.

I continued stroking his head a few seconds longer, my heart settling into its normal rhythm. I convinced Brutus to lie down and stepped over him as I moved to a set of French windows that opened onto a large patio. I was prepared to force the latch, but I didn't need to. The doors were ajar, the tiny catch swinging limply—already broken. I would have given this detail far more consideration if it hadn't been for the dog. This was one of the reasons I had, up to this point, survived so long—because I generally took my time, got to know the comings and goings of my mark, knew the lay of the land so to speak. Acting on impulse was a sure way to get oneself killed, but the expression on the face of Asshole Banker's wife as she fell to her death—that preyed on me more than all of the others combined. The rest had deserved what they got, but that woman's blood was on my hands and I intended to share the sin.

Once inside, I closed the windows behind me and readjusted the curtains so that they looked as they had when I'd entered. I crossed the darkened living room in silence, peeked inside the kitchen and dining room areas then made my way up a set of carpeted stairs. It was on the second floor that my luck ran out.

Along with those unspoken aspects of how Sam and I looked out for one another there were also various rules which we *had* discussed; stuff that had saved our collective asses on more than one occasion. One of the most important was, if separated, let the other guy know if there's trouble. I'd taken two steps down the hallway when I heard a car horn blaring in three long blats—*HONK HONK HONK*—our signal to one another that the gig was up.

For the first time since I'd killed that doctor all those years ago, I stood there frozen, fighting every instinct to simply RUN, to get the fuck out of there as I'd done on other missions when danger had loomed large. This time, I stayed put, and it's probably a good thing I did. Before I made it another step, the bedroom door flew open and a gun was shoved in my face.

"Who the hell are you?" It was a woman, her voice hoarse, as if she'd been crying.

A shaft of light spilled through the open door to the bedroom. The bedside lamp was on, but its feeble glow wasn't enough for me to register her features through the gloom. On the other hand, that light was more than enough for me to catch an eyeful of the nickel-plated .38 she held in her quivering fist.

Behind her, sitting bolt upright on the bed was a middle-aged man and a blonde woman, considerably younger, and considerably *zaftig*. Both were naked to the waist where they clutched at a duvet pulled up tightly against their stomachs. Both had sagging breasts and I had just enough time to think *And you had me ice your wife for* **this***?* when the woman with the gun reiterated her question, this time with the added punctuation of the pistol's hammer clicking back.

"Who—the hell—are *you*?" she asked again, stepping closer. I smelled the mingling odors of gun oil and her expensive perfume.

"I've come to paint the walls," I said. Before she could respond, I reached for her gun, my gloved hand a sooty blur in that shadowed hallway. I took hold of the weapon and gave it a sharp twist, heard the bones in her thin wrist pop out of place. Then the hammer fell.

The pistol's mechanism closed on the soft web of my thumb and, gloves or no, it hurt like a son of a bitch. Probably not as painful as the woman's sprained wrist, but we would both heal. What I'd just done was an idiotic thing to try. Had I counted on it working, I'd probably have ended up with a couple of slugs floating around in my frontal lobe. For this, at least, my luck had returned. Now it was my turn to point a rod and ask questions.

I dropped her gun in my left pocket then pushed her into the room—told her to sit on the edge of the bed so I could keep an eye on all of them at once.

"Anyone else likely to join the party?" I asked.

No one answered.

The next thing I wanted to know was how the woman with the gun had known I was there. "I didn't," she said. "I heard a car horn and thought my ride was indicating a problem."

"I think the message was for me, not you. Speaking of which, who are you, and why are you here?"

The banker opened his gawp to speak, but I shook my head and he closed his mouth so fast his teeth clicked.

"Let's allow the nice lady a chance to tell it."

Now that the woman was closer to the lamplight, I could see that she had left her thirties behind, probably approaching fifty, yet doing so with the grace Mother Nature granted to only a handful. Although a few strands of gray mingled amid her dark hair, and smile lines creased the corners of her eyes, it would be many years before she'd begin to show her true age. She was wearing what I thought of as *sensible clothes*, especially for the work she'd been about to do: a dark waterproof cloak, thin leather gloves, and her hair pulled back with a piece of ribbon. She even wore crepe-soled flats and black stockings. I had to give her credit, because she certainly nailed the role of mysterious *femme fatale*. Tears stood in her eyes and, before she could catch it, one spilled down her cheek ruining her eye liner.

"I'm Margaret. He killed my sister," she sniffed.

I plucked a tissue from a box on the dresser and handed it to her.

"And what were you going to do about it," I asked, "shoot him while he slept?"

"No," she said, flashing a smile so bereft of warmth it stung. "I woke him up so he'd know what he had coming. And *why*."

I watched the woman rub at her aching wrist. I didn't know anything about her, but already I liked her. She had a lot of what the old guys in the neighborhood called *coraggio*. Perhaps she was a tad impulsive, but she had the right idea where her soon-to-be-dead brother-in-law was concerned.

"Listen," I said. "You and I got off on the wrong foot, but I'm going to do you a favor."

"How? By shooting me in the head so I don't feel much pain? This bastard will love that. He might even *pay* you to do it!"

I smiled, but that last bit jabbed at my soul more than she'd ever know.

"Lady, you got me all wrong. I don't work for him. I can't explain all the details, but the fact is you're horning in on my action."

She looked confused.

"What I'm saying is that you need to collect yourself and leave the same way you came in. This matter will play out as it will, and you needn't involve yourself any further than you already have. Go home, get a good night's rest, and read about it in the papers tomorrow."

She held the tissue to her nose and turned to stare at the banker. He and his mistress looked as if they were edging ever closer toward cardiac arrest. "I will not!" she said. "I want to see him suffer!"

I shook my head. "Trust me; you don't. He's not worth all the sleep you'll lose if you stick around to watch."

The banker yelped, and his paramour began to make little hiccupping sounds.

I held out my hand to help the lady to her feet and she took it.

"My sister was everything to me," she whispered.

"I know," I said. "She's the reason I'm here."

The woman nodded, as if she somehow realized that this was so. Another tear spilled creating a parallel streak to match the first. She looked like a mime that some bystander had gobsmacked into imMobility. I squeezed her shoulder, gave her a little nudge toward the stairs, and she disappeared as quietly as I had entered.

22 – *Worse than me*

The rest of the story isn't very interesting. I told the banker's squeeze to get dressed, and took her into the next room where I tied her to a chair and blindfolded her. Then I listened to the asshole himself go through a range of emotions as he pleadingly gibbered, cajoled me with threats, and ultimately begged me to take his secret stash of cash, AND the girl. Most of this was said to me through the adjoining suite while I was busy binding up his love toy. I wanted to leave her out of it, if possible. Other than brief instructions such as "Move here; turn your hands out; close your eyes" and the like, I didn't say anything else. No need, with Mighty Mouth yammering through the doorway.

I eventually got sick of hearing his shit so I jammed my .45 up under this chin and told him why I was there— how I *knew* that the story about his wife had been bullshit— how I'd seen it in her expression when she'd fallen to her death.

"You're still worse than me," he chided. "At least I truly love someone. All you love is..." but he never got a chance to tell me.

And I hadn't lied to Margaret. The walls got
painted with the variegated tones of gore.

23 – *Testament to love*

The banker's Rubenesque girlfriend was a loose end, but I had to trust her good sense not to tell the police too much. She had to have known for whom her lover had worked, and what would happen to her if she ever spilled the beans. I informed her what she needed to tell the cops— how a junkie had broken into the house waving a gun and demanding cash, how the banker got shot refusing to play along, and how the hype had tied her up then proceeded to tear the place apart.

"When should I call them?" she'd asked, voice quavering.

"As soon as you wake up," I suggested just before slugging her unconscious.

It didn't take long to ransack the place. I pretended not to find the suitcase full of large denomination currency on the top shelf of the closet. That's a lame place to "hide" money. Anyone with half a brain would know better, but Asshole Banker was currently missing far more than that. Instead of stealing the dough, I rifled the petty cash out of his wallet then beat it the hell out there.

It wasn't until I closed those French doors that I realized I hadn't heard Sam blowing the horn again. I began to wonder if perhaps I'd been wrong. Had that been nothing more than a coincidence, or maybe Margaret's partner in the dark sedan as she'd supposed?

But my car was still there and Sammy was still sitting in the passenger's seat with the gun resting in his lap.

"What the hell was that horn about?"

Samuel looked at me, eyes sadder than ever, as if he would soon drown under the combined pressures of so much death, and so much blood.

"It took you a long time, Ben."

"Yeah, too long. Let's make like trees and get the fuck out of here."

I started the car, used a neighbor's driveway to make a three-point turn, and was almost a mile away before Sammy answered my question.

"I saw something and beeped the horn."

I didn't reply, not wanting to throw him off.

"There was another car. It circled the block a couple of times and I got worried that maybe it was more guys like us; you know, shooters. Then I saw a nice lady come out the way you went into that house. She waited by the road for a minute and that car came around again. She got inside and it drove away."

I nodded, thinking the situation through. *Who drove the getaway car for her?* I wondered, realizing the kind of trust and devotion necessary to go along with such a scheme. *A lover? Her husband?*

"What did all of that mean, Ben?" Sam asked, and I knew he meant the business with the woman and the car.

"That, my friend, was a testament to love."

24 – *A kind of prophecy*

We ended up back in the neighborhood by 3:00 a.m. I let Samuel off at his mom's house and detoured on the way to my apartment long enough to stop by the local church. I stuck the banker's cash into the alms box and was already beginning to regret my rash behavior. By the time I crawled into bed, I felt like a very bad man indeed. Not for killing the asshole banker, and not for preventing the sister-in-law from performing an act she would soon wish she hadn't. I felt guilty because I'd allowed my emotions to get the best of me, and because, I assumed that, if he knew what I'd done, Papa Theo would be disappointed in me. Worse still, I'd involved Samuel Sloane, selfishly adding to his own burdensome guilt, even if it was only by association.

I laid there in the dark, smoking a last cigarette and thinking to myself that something was going to have to give. "When a guy can no longer stand what he does for a living then it's time to retire," I whispered to myself. I knew this was the way it had to be—either that or give up what little bit of sanity I had left.

I'd had a good run, but it couldn't last forever.

Even the luckiest of bad men have to cash out sometime—

and most shuffle off their mortal coil by being shot in the

head, or by some stranger slitting their throat. I think it was

Bret Harte who said that the only sure thing about luck is

that it always changes. Could as easily have been

Shakespeare; I was too damned rattled to recall. I eventually

fell asleep and dreamt of hitting some kind of jackpot.

There was so much cash it was blowing around in the street.

It wasn't until much later that I came to see that my dream

was also a kind of prophecy.

25 – *The Swordsman*

I said that I never worked with Samuel again, but I didn't mean to imply that I hadn't seen him around. After whacking the banker I kept to myself for a while, but when nobody said boo about it I decided to let it go and eased back into my so-called "normal" life. I took care of business, heard the scuttlebutt from the lieutenants, and went about like usual, an extra pair of eyes for Papa Theo. The boss's other men and I made certain that the neighborhood stayed the quiet little slice of transplanted Italy it had always been.

I still meant to quit, but I wanted to tell Papa Theo face-to-face. After all he'd done for me, I felt I owed him that much. It wasn't going to be easy. Theo had certainly ordered his fair share of evils to be committed on his behalf, and had perpetrated more in his youth, but the man was still a walking talking saint in my book. He could stick a gun in my face and shoot me, I wouldn't think any less of him. Papa Theo had looked out for me the way my own father should have. That counted for a lot more than I could ever repay.

I knew it would also be hard to say goodbye to Sammy, but I assumed he'd figure something out—maybe pack up his mom and skip town with whatever loot he'd saved throughout the years. Despite that thing with answering questions, the kid was no dummy. He was obviously more introspective than the other enforcers could understand, but he had it going on upstairs. The way I saw it, my leaving might be the kick in the pants he needed to quit as well.

The next time that Sam and I met was in front of the local library. We exchanged a few words, which took about fifteen minutes on account of his unusual way of conversing. He was coming out as I was walking in. As much as I liked pulling jobs with him, seeing him there gave me a crawling sensation—my intestines a writhing snake den—making me wonder about a lot of ugly things. I knew next to nothing about him, apart from his proficiency with firearms, but I suspected that Samuel Sloane wasn't one for fiction. Hell, I didn't even know if he could read.

Half a dozen worries went through my mind, most concerning the love of my life who happened to work at that very library branch, until Samuel finally answered my first question, which had been "You checking out books, or girls, paisan?" He said that he was returning a bunch of stuff his mother had borrowed.

"She don't need them no more. She died."

I reached out to touch his shoulder, a gesture of consolation, and Sam flinched. We stood there under that bright, midday sun, a blue sky filled with those wispy clouds that looked as if God had run an old broom through them. Birds flitted by and squawked at us from where they'd built a nest in the loops of the chiseled 'B' in LIBRARY. In between our words, we heard the sound of kids playing in the schoolyard next door, enjoying a well-earned recess. Our shadows were small discs around our shoe leather, barely noticeable under that unwavering light. It hadn't seemed that death could ever touch us—Samuel and I the poster children for good fortune. Yet here it was, having crept up on us just the same, holding dominion over one and all. I could hear its aftereffects rippling through Samuel's morose monotone, as if a stone had fallen into that seemingly still pond his life had been. After a moment of silence, he spoke again, his last two words hanging in the air like a funeral knell rung from St. Mary's a few blocks down the street.

I told Sam that I was sorry about his mom, that I'd liked her, and that I'd help him in any way I could. He gave me a noncommittal sort of nod and turned to leave, then turned back and told me that Papa Theo wanted to see me.

That queasy sensation returned, making me feel as if I'd been punched. I thanked Sammy and told him to call me. Then I went into the library to speak with Veronica, but she wasn't there. One of the clerks said that I'd just missed her, that she'd been called away on a "family matter."

Think me paranoid, but hearing such words in a neighborhood like mine gave me gooseflesh, even on such a pleasant afternoon. Veronica's last name was Barile, an Anglicized version of the Italian moniker of *Barilla*, but she'd come by it from a husband, now long gone. She'd been born a Montresor so, needless to say, she wasn't local and had never been "connected" to the kind of *family* I worked for.

I could play the worried fool and call her, but chances were slim she'd have her phone. V might be obsessed with the written word, and was thus a fan of the Internet, where she often tracked down obscure texts to read, but the woman was a damned Luddite where cell phones were concerned. I gave her one as a gift, yet she seldom used it, insisting I call her landline. I had to know if she was safe, but I'd been summoned by the boss and it wasn't politic to keep him waiting.

Worried fool or no, I dialed Veronica's home number as I walked to my car, muttering "Pick up, baby; c'mon."

No answer.

Hurrying to Papa Theo's place, I felt like my brain was ready to burst; my thoughts now squirming as much as my guts had been. I figured there'd be hell to pay once Theo knew all: not only my having offed the banker, but my desire to quit as well. My quirky meeting with Sammy convinced me that I would never feel secure in my own skin again until I officially "retired" and moved on. Things would look better when I'd gained perspective, but the only way I'd ever get it was by putting a lot of distance between me and this place, this job, this kind of life.

Hearing about the death of Samuel's mom had been unnerving. In one sense, it should have made me feel better about seeing him there, but it didn't. Watching him exit the library while I was going in made me realize the fragility of my own situation—how precarious that balance between life and death —and how guys like me take away the former in the blink of an eye. I suddenly came to grips with how much I truly valued my time with Veronica. I had kept her at a distance because of the job, always the fucking job. She was far more important to me than anything else in my poor excuse for a life, the only person who made me feel wanted, as if I belonged, and I'd do whatever it took to keep her safe.

But back to that thing about the twenty-seven more deaths. Samuel's mom was the first, although I had nothing to do with it. Mrs. Sloane's passing was soon followed by the killing of a couple of guys named Alvin and Carl. Everyone called Carl "Carlito" on account of he was short. I'd never worked with these men, only met them a few times at functions. Neither had struck me as being the brightest bulb in the box, but I guessed that, collectively, they were talented at what they did, which was confidence schemes. Essentially, they were scam artists, but for the boss they mostly handled numbers. Papa Theo had never said a word about either of them to me, and why should he? Regardless, I got the feeling that they'd been given a place in the organization just *because*… Someone owed someone else a favor, or maybe they were quite literally *family*—actually related to the boss in some way or other.

When I got to Papa Theo's home, a guy I'd never seen before ushered me into the boss's office. When Theo looked up, I could see a range of emotions play out across his face; none of them appeared to be anger, but he had never been the type of man to rage in public. More than anything, he looked tired, yet there seemed far more to this than a few sleepless nights—I saw in his eyes something akin to genuine weariness of the spirit.

"Come in, Benjamin. Sit."

I did as I was told, hoping I'd have a chance to give him my spiel about retiring, but as usual, the old man was two steps ahead of me. Of course even Papa Theo understood good showmanship; the power suspense could have on his audience.

"You heard the news—about Carlito, and the other one?"

I hadn't. I shook my head, *No.*

"What is that other fat Dago's name…"

"Alvin," I said.

"Carl and Alvin," Theo nodded, snapping his chubby digits. "They were picking up the sucker bets a few blocks from here when someone walked up to them in the middle of the street—broad daylight this is—and ran them through with a blade. The son of a bitch used a *sword*, Benjamin. An actual *sword*! Do you believe that nonsense?"

My concern for Veronica, combined with my vain wish to tell Theo that my days as an enforcer were numbered, had my mind wandering. I didn't give a rat's ass for either of those dumb wops, God rest and keep their souls, but when the boss mentioned how they'd died, I suddenly felt myself in the *zone*.

An image of how it must have gone down came to me, Carl and Alvin stepping out of Eddie the grocer's, or maybe that little café called The Venice, Alvin in the lead with Carl right on his heels. The assailant approaches, just another customer entering as they are leaving, but then there's the gleam of something bright glinting in the sunlight, and before either man can react, the weapon arcs silently up and forward. Alvin looks down to see a gloved hand wrapped tightly around the weapon's pommel, but he does not fully interpret what he's seeing. He thinks some asshole has punched him in the stomach with some kind of fancy looking bell. Carl is just as confused. He's run into his partner, but he can't back away. It seems as if some magnetic force is holding them together, and, for all intent and purpose this is so. Carl can't quite see the sword's blade over the burgeoning mound of his gut, but he feels both warmth and cold spreading over that tender spot just above his trousers. The swordsman has missed their spines, but rectifies the situation with two swift moves—one takes the blade from side to side, the next yanks it free. Theo's men fall limply to the pavement, their skeletal structure too compromised to support them. Their attacker removes a rag from his pocket, wipes the blade clean, and tosses it between his victims. He enters a taxi that arrives too conveniently for happenstance—this is a getaway car. Carl and Alvin soon bleed out, but the other man is long gone before they do.

Killing with that type of weapon is *quiet*, but flashy. It attracts attention. The perp obviously had panache.

"Anybody see the swordsman?"

Papa Theo nodded, plucked up something off his desk with his sausage-like fingers and handed it to me. It was a photograph of a man I knew. Not personally, but by reputation. A professional bad man. Just like me.

I asked if this individual was a target and the boss laughed.

"Not yours, my boy. You're the best I got, but that man… *He's the best there is.* You've got wisdom, and the tactical thinking necessary to succeed in any situation. That's how you've lasted this long, but you take no pleasure in the work. That fellow in the photograph, on the other hand, he truly *enjoys* killing. I'm guessing that's why he used the blade instead of a bullet to kill those two. He's so good, he gets bored and challenges himself to try new things. Well, that, and he wanted to get my attention."

I mulled this over thinking that Theo could be right. But somehow, I got the feeling that the boss was missing the forest for the trees. For all his powers of observation, his insight into the minds of others, it seemed the killer's point in using a sword might have been symbolic—like he was sending a message, or perhaps it was a warning: *Those who live by the sword...* The meaning might have been overt to the sender, yet as close as I was to the boss, I couldn't figure out how that might apply to Theo. Maybe I was letting my imagination run wild—maybe I'd read one too many detective novels with killers who left such suggestive clues. Leaving notes, or signs of any kind, is *not* a common practice for most guys in the biz. This swordsman might just be an instance of life imitating art.

"If Carl and Alvin's killer is not the target, who is?" I asked, figuring I'd have to pull at least one more job before he'd let me off the hook—especially after my little flourish with the money launderer and his girlfriend.

The boss sighed. He placed his manicured hands on the top of his desk with great delicacy and drummed the meaty pads of his finger tips so softly I could barely hear them.

"I didn't call you up here to send you on a job. Not immediately, anyway. I just wanted you to know that there's something's in the wind. Whatever it is, it don't smell none too good. Vigilance is the key, understand? That's the first part."

I nodded.

"The next thing is Sammy. He told you about his momma, yeah?"

"Uh huh. He mentioned that she was sick last time I saw him, but I never thought…"

A pained expression creased Theo's brow, and deep grooves formed at the corners of his mouth as he frowned. He stared down into the polished surface of his lacquered desk, like he was scrying into a crystal ball. If that was the case, he didn't seem to care much for whatever future he perceived.

"There's something else."

I waited for it, but deep down inside, I guess I somehow knew what he was going to say.

"Sammy's always been a little soft upstairs, but I tell you, the way he's acting lately—the kid's not right in the head. I think the death of his mother has driven him the rest of the way over the cliff. He's threatening to kill me the next time he sees me."

The boss stopped talking, looked up at me, his gaze sleepy, somehow dreamy—the eyes of a romantic. Tears brimmed on his lower lids, suspended, about to fall, but never quite did so. From where I sat I could see another Theo reflected in the dark lacquer of the desk, and that one appeared to be smiling. I was suddenly sure of the awful thing he expected me to do, no questions asked, business as usual. But this was too much. It was simply more than I could stand. It would be like murdering a child.

Before I could open my mouth to argue, Papa Theo said, "I want you to attend the funeral services with me tonight. You'll need a weapon, maybe a backup piece as well. I'll tell you more about the arrangements when I see you later."

Arrangements? I thought. *For Mrs. Sloane, or for her son?*

I got up, not waiting to be told to leave. I needed to get out of that room, to free myself of the cloying sense of impending apocalypse dammed up, yet soon to spill down upon the world. There seemed little likelihood that I'd come out of it unscathed, but I knew I had to try to save as many as I could—Veronica, and Samuel too, if I got the chance.

I made for the door, but Theo had more to say. He didn't launch into it right away, just stared at me, stared *through* me, as if peering as deeply into me as if he were God the Father. I stood there, feeling as if my soul was being weighed, with one hand resting on the back of the chair, my gun hand relaxed and loose at my side. Theo continued to look another thirty seconds then spoke.

"Benjamin, it seems to me as if you're struggling with a problem. You have the look of a man who's begun staring over his shoulder. Those who do so generally do it out of fear, but with you, I sense a kind of resignation—as if you've come to terms with the inevitability of life, and that it always ends, no matter how hard we fight against it."

I nodded, feeling embarrassed to admit such a weakness. Color began to creep up into my cheeks; I swallowed, tried making it go away.

"Papa Theo, I came in here to tell you that I want out."

"I know that, son," he said. "I also know what you did to Hughes."

Hughes—known to me as "Asshole Banker." I knew his name, but had refused to acknowledge it because it made him seem banal, maybe even benevolent, not like the prick he really had been.

"And?" I asked. I tried to swallow, but I had no spit left to do so.

"And, *what*?" the boss asked. "The fellow was a turd. Normally, I would never have considered that contract on his missus, but I had a lot going on. First, that nonsense with Fincino then the Russians. Hughes kept hounding me about it, and I didn't give it the proper attention I might otherwise have done. My mind's been on too many things. A lot of them are now coming to a head. But that's no excuse; I wouldn't accept such a fuck up from anyone else. It was my fault."

I stared at Theo; didn't blink. The boss's admission appeared to be heartfelt. I knew from firsthand experience that Papa Theo took no shit, but he didn't have an inflated ego, like most other dons. He was man enough to admit his mistakes, and I appreciated this aspect about him. Even if he hadn't practically raised me like his own, I couldn't help but love him.

He continued.

"I should not have been so preoccupied, but what's done is done. I do apologize for sending *you* if it makes any difference."

I'd never informed him about what really happened that night. It didn't matter now, but I couldn't keep it from the old man any longer. I told Theo the truth about how the woman had died, about the real accident that took her life. Then I explained how I'd known Hughes had lied, what I'd seen in her eyes just before she fell.

Theo shook his massive head, sighed.

"Then I'm glad for what you did. Just desserts for the bastard. I only wish you'd come to me first. It's difficult to keep such a thing quiet, and if word got out that I had a loose cannon in my employ…"

"I understand. I can disappear quietly, if you like."

"I don't *like*," he said, his voice flat. My heartbeat quickened. "What I mean to say is that it's gonna break my heart to have to say goodbye to you, Benjamin—to see you go."

I relaxed, but only a little. Papa Theo noticed my disquiet and waved his big hands.

"Benjamin, please. You think I'd ever do something to hurt *you*? Goddammit, you're the son I *should* have had. In my eyes… Well, I needn't belabor the point. Go on, get the hell out of here. I'll see you this evening. We'll talk more after Maddy's funeral."

Maddy? But, of course; Samuel's mother. Madeline Sloane.

"Watch yourself," he said.

I gave him a quick nod, said "I will," and left the room. The same man who'd ushered me into the boss's office accompanied me all the way to the foyer, but he never said a thing.

When I was outside, I snatched a lungful of air and realized I'd been holding my breath. On the one hand, I felt relieved, but I could not quiet my mind. Papa Theo's suggestion that I bring an additional sidearm, and his intimation that I might need to use it, were only so much wishful thinking on his part. He'd said I was the best shooter he had, but that simply was not so. That honor belonged to Samuel Sloane. If he sent me to kill Sam then the reprieve for killing Hughes would be a short one. Anyone who found himself on the business end of Samuel's big iron never lived to describe the experience.

26 – *A family matter*

As soon as my ass hit the seat of the car, the sunlight hit my face—ricocheting off the polished hood and blasting into my eyes like molten hot bullets. The air was dry, like desert heat, somehow blown all the way across the plains from cactus country to the big city—the kind of heat that made sensible men do the incomprehensible.

I phoned Veronica, listened to the unanswered rings buzz in a droning monotony through my brain while sweat pricked the corners of my eyes, making me wince. I continued holding the phone to my ear for a full minute then did what every lovelorn sap does—I tried it again.

And again.

She either wasn't home or couldn't answer.

A *family* matter.

My instinct was to act, to do something, ANYTHING. I wanted to drive by V's apartment to make certain that she was okay, to know that Samuel, or another of the organization's thugs, hadn't done her in to keep me in line. But was I overreacting? If I suddenly appeared at her place amid some crisis with her sister or mom, she'd probably be less than happy to see me. Unlike myself, Veronica still had a family, a *real* one, not the kind with ties to drug trafficking, racketeering, and body dumps at 3:00 a.m. in some landfill in Hackensack. For her, a "family matter" might mean that a parent was sick or her brother had been hit by a bus or—

Someone called my name and, for an instant, I was caught off guard, unsure where the voice had come from.

"Hey, Benny! What a, you deaf, o' some-ting'?"

I half-turned, saw the pearlescent gleam of a white arm flapping at me from a nearby storefront. It moved like a limp rag caught in a stiff breeze. The limb was attached to the old man who ran a tavern where Sam and I had occasionally gone after a hit. The fellow was so thin that his white suit hung on his frail bones like pajamas. I blinked a couple of times, but in that blistering light, the man appeared to be an apparition. Just what I needed, yet another ghostly presence.

"Get ina here and drink a some-ting 'fore you cook a you brain!"

Hearing him speak conjured up his name: Bibi Martinelli. He too had been born a *Benjamin*, but had somehow picked up "Bibi" back in the old country. The moniker had stuck, surviving the long transit from Europe to the United States, as had his thick, Venetian accent. He was the only person in the neighborhood who called me "Benny." I'd have shot anybody else for doing so.

I got out of the car, eager for a break from that barrage of sunshine. I winced at every ray arcing off the gleaming chrome from the cars around mine. I entered the dark bar and felt the chilly clamminess of the air conditioning first surround then settle into me. The temperature felt so cool I thought I might see puffs of breath float out when I exhaled. Of course, it really wasn't as cold as all that—just seemed that way after the unexpected heat of the early afternoon.

After a few seconds, my eyes adjusted and some of the soreness dissipated out of them aided by the frigid air. Except for a couple of old guys playing dominoes at a table by the window, the place was empty.

"Why you no hear me when I calla you da firsta time?" he asked, his thick dialect like something out of a bad movie. He fiddled with a TV on the back bar, pulverizing the unit in an attempt to make the image stay put, but it kept rolling no matter how hard he thumped on it.

"Wool gathering," I said.

His brow furrowed, signifying he hadn't understood.

"Dreaming," I told him. "*Sognante.*"

"Ah, si! Who you dream about—*bella donna*?"

"That's right." I smiled, and told him to give me a Coke. He smirked, looked at me like I'd asked for milk, but he placed a bottle of cola in front of me with the same delicacy he'd have given a brimming shot of Jack Daniels.

Bibi was used to the various neighborhood loudmouths coming in, trading barbs with him, shootin' the shit. Apart from a couple of visits with Sammy, I sometimes went in for lunch, but that was it. The smoke and the loud music one usually got with the night-time crowd were not to my liking.

He understood that I didn't talk much, but that never stopped him from flapping his gums in my direction. Perhaps Bibi assumed he had to somehow make up for my own reticence. This day was no exception. He harangued me with his half English/half Italian commentary on the awful state of things in "dis a berry neighborhood!" He was referring to what had befallen those luminaries of good will and human decency, Carl and Alvin. Bibi insisted that they'd been cut down in their prime. And worse still, in front of their own *popolo*.

I nodded, in no mood to argue the pros and cons of those two and their chosen occupation. Nor did I dare to speak ill of the dead in his presence. What Bibi knew, the world soon found out. But the diatribe brought up another issue, as there was obviously an implied subtext: *What are you going to do about it?* Though few people knew the full extent of my responsibilities for the family, it was no secret that I was one of Papa Theo enforcers. I let the matter pass, along with the rest of his prattle. Shaking my head, I said "*Il mondo malvagio.*"

To change the subject I asked about his wife and children and he went into another tirade of bitching, taking out his pent up frustrations on the TV. The more he beat on it, the worse the picture rolled. I asked if I could step behind the counter to look at it and he agreed. I found the little knob on the back of the box, gave it a slight twist and watched the picture flutter then settle back into a steady image. He gave me a pat on the arm then pointed to the screen and asked if I'd heard about the little boy in the well.

I stood there shoulder to shoulder with him, just a couple of guys named Benjamin, squinting at a TV set with a picture no bigger than a slice of bread. The colors were like something out of a horror movie—the newscasters reporting on the trapped child all had purple faces, as if they'd been holding their breath between takes. The grass was bright orange and what little I could see of the sky looked like soot.

"What the hell is this?" I asked.

Bibi explained how some kids had been playing around an abandoned well, over in Queens, and one of them had fallen inside and was hurt. Firemen were trying to get him out, but had, thus far, been unable to do so. The boy was stuck and there wasn't enough room for a grown man to go down inside the opening to free him.

I remembered another well, but that one had been on an old farm outside of Grover's Mill, New Jersey. Samuel and I had tossed a troublesome lump of an Irishman down that hole. The fellow had made disparaging remarks concerning Papa Theo, his wife, his dog, and his sexual prowess, the latter focused on the extent of Theo's interest in the family pet. We had been obliged to demonstrate how much he'd hurt Theo's feelings. I'd meant for the prick to break his neck from the fall, but it had rained a lot and the water table was up. Sam and I heard a splash and then the man himself sputtering and cursing. He didn't beg like most people do, just continued calling us sons of whores and whatever else he could think to sling at us—a lot of it in brogue. I'd shrugged at Sammy, meaning only that none of it mattered, and that he and I should let the fucker drown. Samuel misunderstood. Maybe he thought I couldn't figure out what to do next; this is Sam I'm talking about, so who knows what he was thinking? He stepped to the edge of the well and emptied a full clip down into that dark maw. For a second, I heard the asshole shouting then the echo of gunfire. The rest, as the Bard so aptly stated, was silence.

Samuel Sloane, I thought and shivered, feeling as if someone had just walked over my grave.

"Gotta run, Bibi. Catch you next time around."

I threw down a five dollar bill and Bibi spat.

"You money no gooda here, Benny!"

I gave him a wink.

"Give it to the wife."

"She spenda da 'nough my money!"

I grinned. He grinned back and stuck the cash into his breast pocket.

27 – *Bulletproof plans*

I had a couple more hours to kill before attending the funeral, but I was too worried about Veronica to read, or go see a movie, or partake of any of the little things I usually did while waiting for the action to begin. I would never be satisfied until I checked her place. If she wasn't there, I'd still worry, but it would beat the hell out of finding her dead.

The thought that someone might have killed V— that it was all my fault if they had—once again jumpstarted that loop film of morbidity in my brain. I am a bad man, a death dealer, thus I am cursed to be surrounded by carnage, by mayhem, by a system of cause and effect resulting in ever more chaos and loss of life.

A funeral later. Papa Theo said to bring a piece— maybe a back up as well.

Will there be *action?* I asked myself. *Can I really do what Papa Theo asked?*

I didn't want to think about any of that, but there seemed no way around it. I'd imagined how I might succeed, but it would need to be more than just a solid plan, it would have to be as airtight as Mrs. Sloane's coffin. More than that, whatever I came up with would need to be *bulletproof.*

No matter how slowly Sammy's mind might work while speaking, he didn't need to think where firing his gun was concerned. He was like one of those fancy cameras—just point and shoot. And considering Samuel's speed with a sidearm, I'd need more than any old backup piece. Whatever I brought along must make a *lasting* impression. I stopped by my apartment on my way to Veronica's and snagged an old .45 automatic that I'd rehabbed into working order. The bastard had a kick that could break one's wrist, but it could punch holes the size of silver dollars, in steel, wood, or flesh. Especially flesh. I'd fired it enough times to know its measure and it had never jammed.

This wasn't the route I hoped to follow because, even with two big guns, there was no way for me to outdraw Samuel Sloane, and no way I'd ever get the drop on him without pulling some fancy ruse. The latter wasn't my style, nor was it something I'd ever pull on Sammy. If I had to go up against him, then it would be face-to-face. It was a cinch

I'd lose, but at least I'd ride that down-bound train knowing I'd shown my old partner the courtesy of a fair fight.

I think the boss's reasoning concerning the other weapon was that I wouldn't want to shoot Samuel with the gun I normally used for my other jobs. It had nothing to do with ballistics, yet everything to do with mojo. Papa Theo knew I'd do what I had to, but I guess he assumed it would be easier if I used a firearm I could toss thereafter. One less memory to tote around.

The police sometimes run slugs against known rifling patterns, but they don't always bother with gangland killings. Not that it's much of a problem for guys like me. I don't leave fingerprints on rounds, I collect my brass after a hit, and I generally make the bodies disappear, or have it taken care of by others who are trained in the art of vivisection. On those occasions when I leave a corpse behind, the cops understand that the deceased is left *in situ* as an example. Those who know which side their toast is buttered on steer clear. Such cases are filed as SOLVED and there's an end to it. Ten years of shooting people and I've never switched guns, or been asked to do so.

Until now.

My usual piece was in my shoulder holster, as always. I stuck extra clips in each pocket then folded on old newspaper around the other weapon and headed out the door. I still had well over an hour before I needed to pick up the boss so I risked my sweetheart's ire and swung by her apartment, hoping to find Veronica back from her errand.

It didn't happen.

I knocked half a dozen times, but she didn't respond.

Using my spare key, I opened the lock as quietly as I could, gave the door a gentle push, and crouched low, gun drawn.

Nothing.

Bad vibes swirled in that dim hallway. It was like I was being watched, but I didn't sense anyone inside her place. I know I would have, especially as keyed up as I was at that moment. Even as upset as I was over my girl, not to mention the situation with Samuel, I would have known if another human being was within shooting range. I would have fucking *smelled* him.

I stepped into the living room, hesitated long enough to peer behind the couch then moved from room to room, checking under the beds, in the closets, even in the goddamned shower stall. V's perfume hung faintly in the air like a lilac-scented specter, but I found no other presence in the apartment. No sign of a struggle, nor any indication of where she'd gone, or why she'd left. I got the hell out of there before I invented some other scenario to account for her absence—her *disappearance*.

I drove fast, and made it to The Barker-Gray Cemetery in time for a quick look around. The place had a modicum of fancy masonry work, but mostly small tombstones. The grounds were surrounded on three sides by high walls topped with rusting ironwork, but almost entirely devoid of trees—probably removed years ago—less worry of the roots disturbing those who were peacefully interred. The place had a horseshoe shaped road running around the sides and back. Thus the entrance also served as an exit. Large iron gates were chained back during the day to provide easy access.

The meager acreage was contained within a couple of city blocks, so not a lot of ground to look over. I drove around to the farthest point, got out and walked around examining a couple of the mausoleums—the only structures big enough to provide cover if the shit hit the fan. I saw a crew with a backhoe finishing up a dig, but I didn't see a marker. It might have been for Mrs. Sloane; I didn't stop to ask.

When I returned to Theo's, two of his guys stepped out of the house and motioned for me to park in back. It looked like we'd be riding in style—Papa Theo's black Lincoln Continental, the one with more steel plating than a presidential limo. Having the other men along meant one thing: Theo wanted my hands free for shooting. No driving for yours truly this time around.

A tall fellow, named Owen, held the door open for Papa Theo while the other nearly gave himself a charley horse craning his neck around trying to look in twenty directions at once. The second guy would have made a good owl. All he needed was a pair of wings. I placed myself behind the car and kept my eyes open, unfocused, not looking at any one thing, simply searching for movement. Theo got in and the one holding the door flicked his head for me to follow.

A second later, Owen moved around to the driver's side and slipped behind the wheel. The Owl rode shotgun, bobbing his head this way and that as we pulled out of the driveway and onto the deserted street. I sat across from Theo, facing him from a seat behind the driver, so I could look through the glass behind us. Papa Theo seemed unperturbed, not a drop of sweat visible even though the early evening was still as hot as hell. I didn't like it, but kept my mouth shut. Luxury ride though it might have been, I always thought of that big-ass vehicle as a nothing more than a coffin with fancy wheels, and AM/FM radio.

28 – *I killed her, now you kill me*

Mrs. Sloane hadn't wanted a formal wake in a funeral home, but someone close to her had insisted on at least a graveside service. It might have been Samuel, but I rather doubted it. Probably one of his busybody aunts from up in Poughkeepsie.

There were maybe twenty people standing sentinel-like, quiet except for the occasional sob or sniffle, made up half of relatives and half of locals who'd liked the old lady. Late day sunlight snuck through gaps in the crowd to lick at the polished wood of the casket. The light had a viscous quality about it—yellow and somehow oily. It hurt my eyes to look at it, so I turned my attention back to the faces, searching them for anyone who seemed out of place, and scanning the grounds for sudden movement.

Apart from the boss and the three of us who had accompanied him, there were at least two other men in his employ on hand. They had come in another car a few minutes after we'd arrived. Each one stood nearby, but they didn't mingle with the mourners. I saw Samuel wearing a blue suit that looked at least one size too big for him. He had that same expression as always, as if he'd been dumbstruck with wonder by the simple act of breathing. Who knows? Maybe he was.

I wanted to catch his eye, let him know I was there for him, but his gaze was fixed on the fancy box, which contained his mother's earthly remains. Tears had soaked dark navy spots onto his lapels. I watched his shoulders heave up and down, but he never uttered a sound.

A robed figure separated himself from the throng. Father Merluzzo. The priest began with a brief benediction: "Lord God, whose days are without end and whose mercies beyond counting, keep us mindful that life is short and the hour of death unknown. Let your Spirit guide our days on earth in the ways of holiness and justice, that we may serve—"

The father's words were cut short by the sound of bullets caroming off tombstones. Relatives screamed and ran, momentarily blocking my view. I saw the priest take a round in the leg and fall, nearly toppling over onto the coffin. Every wiseguy there was either on the ground or scrambling for cover. I grabbed Papa Theo and shielded him until we could get behind a mausoleum. The structure was capped with the statue of an angel carrying a horn—Gabriel, I guessed, hoping it wasn't a sign of the judgment to be pronounced upon us for our various transgressions.

Two more shots whined off the windshield of the hearse and another blasted a finger from the angel above our heads. I remember thinking the loss was going to make it difficult for him to blow that trumpet—another sign? The dismembered digit thudded in the dirt between Theo and me, pointing back toward the gate through which we'd come in. I calculated the geometry of those shots, triangulating their point of origin, and knew it must have been from just outside the fence near the entrance. *Always trust your guardian angel*, I mused.

With the exception of the grave markers, there was simply nowhere else to hide. I asked the boss if he had a piece. He nodded and withdrew a small caliber Beretta from inside his suit. I nodded then rolled away from our place of concealment, moving toward the back of the cemetery. Crouching low, I moved down one row of stones and up the next, zigzagging back and forth while the asshole shooters sprayed the place with lead. Packed earth and fresh-mown grass exploded around my feet. A sliver of stone grazed the upper thigh of my right leg, but I hardly felt it; too much adrenalin. I kept going until I reached the wall; no place left to go but up. With no other options at hand, I stepped on a small monument and jumped. I snagged the top of the wall with my finger tips and scraped a good pair of wingtips to ruin trying to boost myself high enough to gain a solid purchase. Another round zinged close to my position, but there was nothing I could do except pray I didn't get shot in the ass while I hung there straining to get to the top.

My present angle was partially covered by a monument in the shape of a draped urn, although I guessed it didn't provide the immortality it symbolized. Still, there'd be no way to get a clear shot at me until I was near the top of the wall, but by then it would be too late. I got a leg up, made it the rest of the way onto the wall, and felt a puff of hot wind touch the back of my neck as a bullet creased the air three inches from my head. I cleared the row of spiked rails atop the wall and dropped to the other side, landing on a patch of spongy grass. I kept to the lawn as much as I could to deaden the sound of my footfalls and quickly covered the distance to one corner and approached the next. Before rounding the second one, my weapon was already in my hand. I did a quick check and saw exactly what I assumed I'd find: four men. One of them waiting in a car, the other three kneeling near the gate, taking shots at anything that moved. Were these guys for real? So far as I knew they hadn't hit anyone except Father Merluzzo. Who the hell would hire such fuck ups? Even Fincino's goons had been more on-the-ball than these clods.

Figuring out who had sent them would come in time, but first I needed to stop them from killing the boss. There were only small shrubs and a sickly looking tree between myself and them, but as intent as they were on playing carnival shooting gallery, I didn't figure they'd see me until it was too late.

The driver was puffing on a cigar, and happened to glance up into his rearview mirror. He was the first of them to see me. He turned to look, his eyes growing wide as his hand came up, about to lay on the horn. I put a bullet through his right eye. His body hitched up in the seat, then he began to sag slowly forward.

At the sound of my shot, the other three turned. The driver fell on the car horn and startled their attention away from me for a fraction of a second. I took out the closest with a slug through the heart. I aimed at the next one, but his body was slammed back out of my line of fire by a round from inside the cemetery. The other guy tried to run, but I was on him before he could get to his feet. I kicked him in the temple and he lost his pistol. He curled up trying to protect his head. I let him. Instead I put a toe into his ribs and heard the wind whoosh out of him.

Then the Owl was there, his head bobbing and weaving, searching the car, the street, the fucking sky, as if maybe more shooters would come parachuting in. He got the man I'd kicked, helped him to his feet and led him away. For a second I felt sorry for the schmuck. He'd be made to talk. He would swear, he would plead, and soon enough, he would cry. He would ultimately wish he'd never been born, maybe even curse his parents for creating him in the first place. He would die whimpering, and then he would disappear, tossed into the East River, dissolved with acid, or ground to paste in a wood chipper. I looked around wondering who'd capped the other guy before I could get off another round. I saw Sammy standing there, his suit grass stained and covered with leaves. He held a chrome-plated Smith and Wesson police special at his side.

"That was nice, Samuel. Fast and clean, as always."

He nodded, but I didn't think he was acknowledging my comment; it seemed like he was listening to some other voice—an otherworldly presence that only he could hear.

"So many bad men," Sammy said. He looked up at me and I saw more tears standing in his eyes. "I'm going to kill Papa Theo now."

"You, *what*?" but before I could say anything else he turned and ran back into the cemetery, toward the very place where I'd left the boss.

"Sammy, wait!" I said, but it was no use, he was hauling ass back up that long drive, and was six or eight paces ahead before I could get myself in gear.

Running after him, I kept thinking *This isn't the way it should go down. I want to save his ass, not shoot him.* There had to be a way to get Sam the hell out of New York and make it look as if I'd killed him. But if he simply wouldn't budge, I'd envisioned several options for getting rid of him, the most logical being to offer him a lift home then drop him with a shot to the back of the head; dead before he ever made it to the curb. Such a plan might have worked if A) I didn't miss, B) he wasn't packing heat of his own, and C) if I hadn't already promised myself that Sam and I would square off on even terms. I knew I the latter option was little more than a pipe dream because we were definitely *not* equal where marksmanship was concerned. Imagining Samuel with a gun, well, I think I've made it clear enough what he could do with a weapon.

Now all of that was a moot point.

Of all the scenarios I *had* imagined, none of them included Sam wigging out and going after the boss; but then I hadn't been in the best frame of mind for quite some time. Theo was right—I was losing my edge, had in fact, already lost it. Technically, it wasn't my job to scout locations for meets and events like the graveyard, but I *had* done so, had seen the situation with that single entrance and exit, and had blithely gone along with it. I should have secured a definite avenue of escape for Papa Theo before allowing him to set foot in that place. Any dumbass could have seen that sending him into what amounted to a *cul de sac* might prove disastrous. And, yet again, that dumbass was me, with my head wedged firmly up my butt. There was no excuse for it, except...

Except, who was I kidding? No matter how well protected a don might seem, if someone wants him to vanish then it's only a matter of time before it happens. Might take days, months, or years, but some joker will eventually pull it off.

But now, Sammy. Damn him. I'd hoped to pull off a disappearing act, make it look like I'd sawed him in half, or made him vanish—POOF! all gone forever; a trick worthy of Houdini. Knowing I couldn't best him with a gun, the idea lodged in my head to try and save the goof—to get him far enough away that no one would bother him—maybe set him up in a little job somewhere. I could find the body of some other sap to take his place, and Samuel Sloane departs from *this* world to be reborn elsewhere, with no one the wiser.

I thought of something Veronica always said to me when things didn't work out, how Robert Burns had it right when he'd written about "the best-laid schemes o' mice an' men."

Accompanying that thought was the realization that I was neither a *mouse* or a *man*—I was the wolf in sheep's clothing. I was Sammy's "bad man"—a predator that walked on two legs, with a gun for my claws, and bullets for fangs. Now he was my prey and the only thing that made it seem even vaguely fair was that he had a gun of his own and could shoot back.

"Samuel, wait!"

He ignored me, continually pulling farther and farther ahead. No way I could keep up with those long legs—not with all the smoking I'd done.

"Hey!" I called. "What the fuck's the matter with you?"

My gun was still in my hand. The cool weight of it in my sweating fist felt reassuring, but not nearly enough in light of the situation. It might have been simpler to stop, take aim, and pop Samuel right then and there, but even with my thoughts in such a muddle I had brains enough to know that the place was lousy with witnesses; certainly not the way the boss would have wanted it done. Killing Sammy like that would have meant killing all of the bystanders, maybe even the priest. *I could do it*, I thought then chuckled to myself for even considering such insanity. Even if I'd wanted to, I didn't have enough ammo for such an undertaking.

Samuel finally reached the large tomb where the newly amputated angel still struggled to play a tune that would bring down the house. Sammy tried to slow himself on the slick grass, but went down with an "Oomph!." I saw a flicker of steel and realized he'd dropped his piece. A couple of seconds later I was on him, my weapon jammed into his forehead, just above the bridge of his nose. We were both wheezing from the exertion. Sammy kept mouthing something, but he couldn't get in enough wind to make himself heard. I knelt down and moved the gun under his left armpit.

"What… are you… trying… to say?" I gasped.

Sam sucked in a lungful of air and finally blurted out, "I killed her!"

Huge tears welled up in his melancholy eyes, so large I briefly saw a reflection of myself, upside down within them. He blinked, creating salty rivulets as they ran down the sides of his face to pool in his ears.

"I killed her," he repeated. "So now you can kill me."

That creepy feeling I'd had all day suddenly returned, bright red in my imagination—a hellish bit of ESP. I felt the muscles in my jaw tense as I clenched my teeth, felt my molars ache under so much stress.

"Killed *who*?" I shouted.

Of course Sammy couldn't answer me—not just like that—not without giving my question time to rattle around in his addled fucking brain. I knew this, but I couldn't help myself. I drew back the hammer on my weapon and pressed the muzzle hard enough into his tender flesh to make him squirm. "WHO?"

Samuel only nodded, mumbled "I killed her, you kill me; it's only fair." His eyes kept leaking as he stared up into mine, imploring me to pull the trigger and be done with it. I withdrew the gun, stuck it back in its holster and waited, but Sammy didn't say anything else. He turned his face to one side and continued to sob.

29 – *The lamb, not the lion*

Nearly everyone has acknowledged, at one time or another, how there's never a cop around when you need one. This was a time when we definitely didn't need the law crawling up our collective asses, but they showed up just the same. A couple of rookies arrived on the scene, made the rounds of the attendees, berating people with questions, jotting down whatever useless crap Mrs. Sloane's distant kin babbled out, but the folks from the neighborhood all sang the same tune: "I heard the shots, officer, but I didn't see a thing."

Someone had had the good sense to get the boss into his limo before the badges appeared on the scene. Papa Theo was still in his car when they arrived. He made no move to get out and greet them, leaving all of that to the Owl and one of the other men. I'd had my hands full with dodging bullets and shooting back, but I should have thought about Papa Theo's safety first. Just goes to show you how focused I was—only on all of the wrong things. At least we were shut of the drama of Samuel and I doing the quarter-mile dash before the cops showed up.

And before those bright-eyed boys in blue could get around to the rest of us, a captain named McCammon arrived, told the naïfs to get the mourners out of the cemetery in an orderly fashion—dismissing them to what amounted to traffic detail. The patrolmen weren't exactly pleased.

Any other time, I might have laughed, but I saw a glint in the old cop's eye, a spark I'd seen in more than one lawman's gaze—one that said *payoff*, transmitted to me on a psychic wave, as if written on the wind in bright neon dollar signs. The captain ambled over to the boss's ride, got in, and they talked for maybe ten minutes. A lot of greenbacks changed hands, and soon after, a meat wagon came to collect the bodies, and a wrecker hauled away their vehicle. McCammon explained the situation to his men—a couple of former altar boys who had it in for the priest—and that was that.

The service was over before it had ever had a proper chance to begin. The grounds crew was already shoveling dirt into the open grave when Theo's car pulled up next to me and the Owl told me to get in. I inquired about

Samuel. The boss explained that he'd asked a couple of the other fellows to take him home.

I wondered about that.

Papa Theo must have seen the worry in my face. He looked at me, weary to the bone, but he managed a smile. "No need to worry, Benjamin. I understand that Samuel's your friend. I know you'll want to help him through this any way you can."

He looked down at the grime on the knees of his slacks, the dirt under his fingernails. I was willing to bet that such a thing was a rare sight. It had been many a decade since Theo had had to get his hands dirty in any literal sense. The old man shook his head, his jowls swaying. "It's too bad, really. The poor kid's never been very bright, but after the last couple of assignments some of the boys said they caught him looking into mirrors and talking to himself. He kept saying something about being a sinner and repeating 'There is no one righteous, not even one'—crazy shit like that."

"That's from *Romans*," I said, "must be something his mother taught him."

"Interesting," said Theo.

I couldn't stand it any longer—I had to know what the hell was going on, and fast.

"Papa Theo, I mean no disrespect, but I need to know who Samuel killed. He kept saying 'I killed her, I killed her.' Who the hell was it?"

The boss looked surprised. At first I thought it was astonishment over my audacity, that after all these years of patiently listening and observing, I had finally crossed the line and spoken out of turn. But the expression turned to one of compassion wrinkling the flab on his forehead.

"You really don't know?" he asked. My eyes widened, but my throat was too dry to speak. I didn't even dare to shake my head *No*.

"His own mother, Benjamin. Samuel killed Madeline Sloane."

I couldn't believe what I was hearing. I was expecting a name, fearing it would be that of someone I held dear, but not this. This seemed too impossible—anathema to everything Samuel stood for in this world.

"Sam shot his own mother?"

The boss gave me a sidelong glance. "Of course not. She'd been very ill. He was helping her down the stairs when she slipped and fell. It was obviously an accident, but he blames himself. He's in pain, Benjamin, and he's no longer thinking straight. He needs to be put down."

I relaxed back into the seat, *collapsed* truth be told, feeling like somebody had kicked me in the balls. Relief, anger, even a giddy sort of hilarity raced through me while I sat there staring out the back glass, seeing everything, taking in nothing. My expression remained a passive mask and I didn't say anything else until we got back to Papa Theo's. Even then there wasn't much to talk about. I asked the boss if he had anything particular in mind concerning Sammy, or if he wanted me to handle it my own way.

He shrugged, sighed, turned his hands up indicating *Non capisco*.

"I'll do it soon," I said.

Theo gave me an approving nod then pressed a button on his intercom. He said, "Bring me the newspaper." A man entered carrying a copy of *The Times*, looked to Theo, who pointed in my direction. The guy handed it to me and when I caught the heft of it I knew my other .45 was wrapped inside. The man left the room without being told.

"You showed quick thinking tonight," the boss said. "Otherwise we might not be having this conversation. You even brought this fine piece as I'd asked, but I'm curious, Benjamin... Why did you leave it inside the car? Why didn't you carry that one as well?"

There seemed to be a thousand reasons, the least of which was that I hadn't actually received precise instructions about what to anticipate. Nor had Papa Theo explained how he wanted the situation handled where Samuel was concerned. The extra weapon had seemed an odd request, but I'd worked it out that he might have wanted me to use it to whack Sammy at some point after the ceremony. I was uncomfortable with the idea of doing such a thing on impulse, but more to the point, there was no way I could have killed a friend on hallowed ground; I was also uncomfortable with trusting that sidearm over my regular piece. More than anything, I assumed there would be more time.

He smiled, seeing that I understood the full import of the situation, like he could somehow read my thoughts.

"I see from your expression that you think you know what I'm going to tell you, but you don't. Everyone has an off day, Benjamin, even you, but this is something else entirely. If you're honest with yourself, you'll admit another possibility in addition to those motivations that have just passed through your mind. You will concede that you no longer have the stomach to do the job. A headshrinker would say you left that gun behind so you could avoid the inevitable."

A dark moment stretched out between us. As cruel and heartless as Papa Theo seemed, I knew the cold blooded son-of-bitch was right. Hadn't I been plotting other contingencies? Even ways to spare Sam's life? This was not like me. I always knew my options, but I never allowed my personal opinion to enter into the equation—not until I offed that ballsack, Hughes. I did my job efficiently, and without stopping to consider whys and wherefores, only those factors pertinent to performing my task and getting away unscathed, and unseen.

This time, I anticipated what Theo was about to say next, that I was far too close to the situation and that one of the other enforcers should do this, but I didn't want to hear it. I couldn't let him take the opportunity away from me.

"You need to let me do this," I told him.

The boss considered, weighing the possibility in his mind as if examining it for holes.

"I love you, Benjamin, so you will forgive my skepticism. Why should I believe you will succeed?"

I wanted to smile, but didn't. "Because I'm the only one who can. Unless you send a dozen guys to raid the place you'll never kill him. Even then, you'll lose three-quarters of them before it's over. Like you said—I'm the best you've got."

Papa Theo tapped his fingers ever so delicately on his desk, touching the wood in that way which was his habit. He did so very lightly, never using his nails, the pads of his fingertips almost silent.

"When you finish with Samuel I want you to return here."

"Another job?" I asked.

"No, my son, you do this for me, and you're finished. Do what you do so well then come back so I can say goodbye."

Our eyes met and, this time, his seemed to be smiling. Too soon, I saw sad understanding reappear in them, spread across his face like a pall, but whether that play of emotions was for me, or the task before me, that I couldn't know. I opened the newspaper, looked at the other gun and wondered if I could really do it: not the act of shooting Samuel Sloane, to that I was now committed, but whether or not I could go up against his speed and accuracy and come out of it alive. Still, it was better that his best friend should do the hit than some stranger. At least I cared enough about him to make it painless—for him, anyway.

With the .45 tucked in the paper's ratty folds, I hit the bricks feeling as never before that what I was about to do was genuinely a mortal sin—one for which the Lord God, Jesus Christ, my Savior, could ever understand or reprieve. *More blood*, I thought, *but this time it's going to be the lamb's and not the lion's.*

30 – *Dreamy, but at peace*

Do I need to describe the seven kinds of hell I went through walking out of there en route to kill my friend? It crossed my mind to just get in my car and drive the fuck away, but I knew I wouldn't—that I absolutely could not leave the task incomplete. Never before had a job gone unfinished, and this was one assignment that *had* to be— done, finished, over. Otherwise, there was no way that Papa Theo was letting me off the hook.

And I've told the truth about everything up to now, so I might as well spill this part as well. I figured that none of it really mattered—not in the overarching scheme of things—because, I assumed, that even if I somehow managed to shoot Samuel (not likely, but I could always hope) then not long after, someone would be waiting to pick me off. Maybe even the boss himself.

He'd asked me to return after the hit so he could say "goodbye." All I could think of was that old novel by Raymond Chandler, *The Long Goodbye*. Depending on what Theo had in mind, that title might prove my epitaph.

I'd had a viable plan for nearly every job I'd ever pulled, even the very first one. Plotting ahead of time what I would do and how I would get away; casing the location, knowing schedules, and taking into account all the myriad loose ends I might encounter in pursuit of my prey. That was the way I'd always worked. But this time, the *last* time, I had jack shit in the way of preparations.

But I didn't hesitate. If I waited, I'd overthink the problem, psyche myself out, try some half-assed play that might result in more destruction of life; the deaths of other family members—my own included—or innocent bystanders who had the misfortune to get in the way. I got in the car, tossed the extra piece on the passenger's seat, and aimed the car in the direction I needed to go.

I drove to Sammy's, parked on the street, and sat there staring at my weapon, the one in my holster, not the other one Papa Theo had supposed I'd use to assuage the emotional connection. I contemplated all of the things I've previously described—especially that part about damnation and doing myself instead. At one point, I even thought about driving back to shoot the boss, hearing a brief echo of Sam's own voice saying "I'm going to kill Papa Theo now."

I'm not sure how long I sat like that, maybe twenty minutes. I could have sat there a month and I still wouldn't have had any better idea of doing what I had to do.

"Fuck it," I said, got out of the car, tucked the newspaper with the extra weapon under my arm, and walked right up and knocked on Samuel's door. It was slightly ajar, and moved when I'd rapped my fist against it. Without waiting for a reply, I opened it the rest of the way and let myself in.

A single lamp was on in the living room off the foyer. The soft illumination made lumpy shadows of the furniture. I heard Samuel say "Hello, Ben" and nearly pissed my pants. I hadn't realized how tense I'd been until that instant when he nailed me to the spot with a simple greeting.

One of the shadows moved and another light came on. Sam was sitting at one end of the couch, still dressed in that ill-fitting suit. I saw a couple of spots of blood on the left lapel and realized at least one of Theo's men had popped him in the jaw hard enough to bust his lip. They'd dared to do that much, but not to draw a gun on him. The boss might not have a crew of geniuses working for him, yet they are obviously smart enough to know that none of them are fast enough to beat Samuel. Yet even while roughing him up as they had, I bet the kid never said a word.

Sam had his hands in his lap, which left them in a murky penumbra thrown from the sofa's camel back. I assumed he had a gun. I would have had one too if I knew the boss was sending an ace to deal me out. *Too late to worry about that*, I thought.

"You know why I'm here," I said, taking a few steps toward him. The newspaper folded around the .45 felt awkward. I took the bundle into my left hand, but didn't open it, knowing it was stupid to have brought it along in the first place. I realized now that I'd never have time to draw either weapon before Sammy shot me to pieces.

"It's okay, Ben."

Those words, as if he was acquiescing to the whole she-bang. My heart sank and I felt tears sting the corners of my eyes. I had to do it now and fast. Draw the gun, pull the trigger, *finito*, over with. But something held me back. Somehow I wanted him to understand why this was happening and to realize…

To realize what? That this wasn't *my* fault?

I let out a sigh. He looked up at me, his expression filled with even more grief than usual. This was definitely *my* fault. What I needed to get across to him was that it wasn't *his*.

"Samuel, listen. You didn't kill your mother. Do you understand?"

He nodded, shook his head. *Yes. No.* Then I realized he wasn't answering my question. He'd come to a far more intimate conclusion based on some inner debate. As usual, no one except Sammy could comprehend what that might be.

I could have moved, leveled the automatic and put two neat holes in his chest, but the gun suddenly felt too heavy, as if it now carried the weight of all the life it had taken throughout the years. There was no way in hell I could shoot Sammy. No way.

"We need to figure this out," I said. I placed the newspaper on the table between us meaning to sit down in the chair opposite. There had to be an out for him somewhere, some manner in which to spirit him away. If there was such a thing as justice in this world, I would find a method by which to spare him.

I turned, looking around at the film of dust that had collected on the shelves in the few short days since his mom had passed. You hardly ever notice little details like that—how hard a person works to keep a home looking good—I saw movement reflected in the glass covering the print of an angel. The heavenly messenger had this strange look on its face, like it was at total peace, the evils of the world be damned. There was a sharp click and I turned to see Samuel holding the .45 I'd so conveniently laid before him.

"I wanted you to kill me at the graveyard so I could die and be with my momma, but you didn't. I know why."

"Why is that?" I asked, more to keep him talking, hoping I could duck behind a chair and give myself a moment to grab my holstered piece.

"It was me that killed her, Ben. No one else was here. She was yelling at me. She kept saying I did terrible things. I wanted to hold her and show her I was still her little boy, to show her how much I loved her. I didn't want her seeing me as a bad man. I only wanted to give my mom a good home 'cause she couldn't work."

He turned slightly, and I saw tracks of moisture gleam on his face. He didn't wipe them away, and his arm never wavered. He kept the gun aimed directly at my head.

"Momma tried to move away from me and she slipped. She fell down the stairs before I could catch her. I ran down and picked her up. A bunch of her bones was broken. I could feel them moving around, but she wasn't dead. She was wheezing and blood was coming out of her mouth. Funny how all the other blood I've seen never mattered, but seeing her blood made me afraid. Her eyes was big, like in a cartoon. I thought at first she was scared of me then she said 'Please,' and I knew what she wanted me to do."

I said "Samuel," but he ignored me and kept talking.

"I put my hands around her neck and snapped it as easy as killing a bird. I saw her spirit fly away. I wanted to follow her, but you didn't kill me like I wanted you to. You couldn't shoot me because you're not a bad man, Ben. Not like me. You're just good at what you do."

I stood there, my own eyes filling with tears, my hands out at my sides like I was trying to balance myself on a frozen lake. I was standing on ice alright, and it was pretty damned thin. I felt the painful surge of my heart trip hammering through my fingertips, the blood singing "SHOOT HIM, SHOOT HIM, SHOOT HIM" in my ears in syncopation with every throbbing beat.

"We'll figure something," I said, taking a step back. "Let's get the hell out of here. What do you say, my friend?"

"I wish you'd shot me," Samuel repeated, his voice wistful and far-away. I knew I'd never get a better chance. I crouched slightly to launch myself behind a cabinet full of bric-a-brac, but I never made it. There was a deafening BOOM and something hot punched me in the shoulder. I was thrown back onto an end table, the legs snapping out from under me, a lamp flying off to shatter near my face in a blistering array of sparking filament.

I rolled onto my side, saw a dark stain expanding across the upper quadrant of my coat. My right arm wouldn't move. By force of habit I tried lifting myself with it anyway and a blast of orange light lit up my brain. The pain was significant enough to make me nauseous. I felt cold tendrils lacing through my synapses, saw brilliant electrical static fill my field of vision and knew I was going to black out unless—

I used the other arm, made it to my knees, tried reaching for my .45 with my left hand, but got tangled in my coat. I almost fell flat on my face, but caught my balance on an armchair. Samuel was somewhere behind me.

My brain kept telling my legs to move, to turn me around and face him, even if it was just to take whatever else was coming, what I deserved for acquiescing to this fool's errand. But that wasn't happening. Somewhere between the command to move and actually doing so, the connecting mental thread had short-circuited, fried to ruin like that burst bulb a moment before. *Then it's to be execution-style*, I thought, figuring Sammy was probably standing over me, already set to send another round through the back of my skull.

He muttered something behind me. This was followed by another loud report. The sound goaded me to action and I jumped to my feet and turned. Sammy was still sitting at the end of the sofa. Blood and bits of bone were sprayed across the wall behind what was left of his head. His eyes seemed to be fixed on mine. His expression looked just like that of the angel in that kooky painting—dreamy, but at peace.

31 – *A well of nothingness*

I felt drunk as I staggered from the house of the late Samuel Sloane. I thought at first it might be from blood loss, but it didn't take long for the flow of my bodily tissue to slow and clot over. I stuffed my handkerchief into the wound and my vision momentarily blurred from the gut wrenching pain. My arm still wouldn't move, but that had more to do with the force of the blow—the kind of numbness one feels from hitting an elbow, only magnified a thousand fold. I didn't think anything was broken and I found out later that the bullet had only nicked the bone. The local doctor, a fellow who often patched up guys who found themselves on the wrong end of guns, and lived to tell about it, explained to me that the round hadn't even come close to an artery. "The guy who shot you must have known what he was doing," he'd said.

"How's that?"

"Well, at the range you say, if he'd wanted to kill you it's pretty obvious how easily he could have."

So true, I thought.

Samuel had saved my life yet again, knowing I couldn't kill him, providing me with a sort of alibi, a badge of blood I could wave in everyone's face while saying "Look, you bastards, I won."

Except the truth of the matter was that I'd lost—one of the few people I cared about had been reduced to little more than worm food, and there was no one left, but me, to mourn him.

The doctor offered me pain pills, but I didn't take them. I'd earned this the old fashioned way and I didn't want anything to take away from that experience. Because of me, a good man was dead. No matter what Samuel thought of himself, I knew the real story—at least I thought so.

Resolved to take the rest of my medicine in one walloping dose, I returned to Papa Theo's. An ambulance passed as I turned onto the street and, for the second time that day, I felt a goose walk over my grave. I started into the house, but a barrel-chested little fuck whom I'd never seen before put up a hand and asked where I thought I was going.

"Papa Theo sent me on a job. He said he wanted to see when it was done."

"Theo aint seein' nobody tonight, not tomorrow night, and not the night after that."

My right arm twitched and I winced. If not for the numbness I'd have drawn my weapon and decorated the ceiling with this fucker's brains—maybe see how close I could get to matching the pattern of spatter that Sammy had left behind.

I opened my mouth to tell this idiot how far up his ass I was going to cram his head when someone stepped between us saying "Whoa! Whoa! What's going on here?"

It was the Owl. He looked at the short fuck, jogged his head around to me, back to the little guy, and then to me again.

"Jesus, man! What the hell happened to you?"

"Quit wasting my time," I said. "Tell the boss I want to see him."

"Riz here wasn't messin' with you. The boss can't see nobody. He's *dead*."

I looked at the Owl and thought *What large eyes you have!* my brain mixing in the words from a children's story I could no longer recall the name of. The hallway leading into the house had felt almost claustrophobically small when I'd first walked in. Now it suddenly seemed miles wide. Where the walls met the floor I could see the baseboard shifting out of true, then I lost my balance. I said "Theo's gone?" and fell headlong into a bottomless well, black, and filled with all the nothingness of the universe, and the dimensions beyond.

32 – *A gorgeous piece of work*

When I came to, I was in bed. It wasn't one that I recognized. I pushed myself up and groaned as the ache in my shoulder pulsed like a strobe light. It felt as if someone had tried to chop it off and had left the axe buried in my sinews. God, it hurt.

On a table next to the bed stood a pitcher of water and a bottle of aspirin. I tried to pop the cap, but dropped it in the process. The door was opened by someone I recognized. I didn't remember his name, but he was one of the big shots I often saw whispering into the boss's ear during those functions I'd attended.

"Feeling better?"

"No, but thanks for asking. What happened to Papa Theo?"

He frowned and his mouth puckered in on itself. And like that, I had his name: *D'Amato*. It was that weird look that did it—*D'Amato the tomato*—that's how I thought of him. Strange face or no, D'Amato was one of the few lieutenants who didn't flaunt his authority. I was pretty sure he was Theo's *consigliere*, or at least next in line in case of such a contingency. He shook out a few pills and handed them to me. I didn't count them, just swallowed the lot with a sip of water.

I asked if he'd mind pouring me another glass. He smiled and did so. Truth was I was so damned thirsty I wanted to down the entire pitcher full. I drank the second glass and repeated my question.

"Someone murdered him."

"Who?"

D'Amato made that face again and ran his fingers over a thin mustache. I wanted to tell him that a tic like that made him look nervous, which he obviously was, and that he'd find it difficult to generate respect doing such a thing. I let it slide. He would soon be someone else's problem, not mine.

"You heard about what happened to Carlito and Alvin, right?"

I nodded.

"We think it was the same guy."

"You *think*?"

He gave me a look as if to say he didn't care for my tone, but I was beyond worrying about what he might like or not. I didn't work for him. I didn't owe him, or the organization. Not one more damned thing.

"Hey, Joey!" he called. The man who'd driven Theo's car came into the room carrying something at his side.

"Show him," D'Amato said.

Joey raised the item and extended it before him with both hands, like he was offering it to me for appraisal. It was a sword.

The thing was a gorgeous piece of work. An Italian *spade*; a rapier-like weapon, well-balanced. It was more plain in appearance than its French cousins, yet nonetheless stunning. The mirrored surface of the steel glinted in the sunlight. Here and there I could see what looked like tiny rainbows along the length of the blade where the oiled metal created a prismatic effect.

"The guy used this on the boss?"

"Not that we could see," he said.

D'Amato nodded and Joey took the sword out of the room. I wanted to ring both of their necks for keeping me in suspense. I raised my eyebrows, but said nothing. D'Amato squirmed.

"What the fuck you want from me, Balsamo?"

Ah, I thought, *every wiseguy in this family knows my real name, but this kingpin still thinks I'm Italian.*

I waited for him to spill it, too pissed off to let him off the hook.

"We found Theo slumped over his desk with this thing in his hand."

"Anything else?"

"Yeah, a note. It said *Theodore Malandra lived and died by this*."

33 – *The earth abideth*

Like Papa Theo before him, D'Amato didn't comprehend the metaphor. I had gotten it when the other two were killed, yet although I'd seen it as a message, I hadn't warned Theo that he was obviously the prime target.

And no matter what the other members of the organization might believe, I got the feeling that this situation was far from over. Someone willing to live by the sword and risk dying by it himself (a man who, if the boss had been right, actually *enjoyed* killing) was not a person that the family should trifle with. This was the type of guy for whom the term *scorched earth* had been invented.

D'Amato asked if I'd like to do another job once I'd healed. I wanted to laugh, but said that I'd think about it.

Before I left, D'Amato handed me an envelope with my name on it. I had no idea if he knew about my arrangement with the boss, how I wasn't coming back. He probably did. I drove home and used my good hand to dial Veronica's number. If Samuel hadn't killed her, and Theo hadn't held her as a carrot to lead me on, then where the hell was she?

The phone rang.

No one answered.

I couldn't stand it. *Someone* had to know *something*. I placed my gun in my jacket pocket, the shoulder holster no good to me as long as my right arm was out of commission, picked up my keys and moved toward the door. I was determined to use whatever means necessary to find out what had happened to my girlfriend, even if it meant shooting more people in the process. I swung open the door and there she stood, her fist raised.

"Hey! I was just about to knock!"

I felt that woozy sensation creep back over me and I saw Veronica's expression turn to concern.

"You okay?"

I hugged her to me with my good arm and kissed her hard. After a couple of minutes she leaned back and asked if we could take it inside. She shut the door behind us and I pelted her with questions, asking where'd she'd been and why she hadn't telephoned.

"My sister called, out of her mind, begging me to come and help. Her son fell down a well and was stuck there for hours before the fire department cooked up an idea to get him out."

"I heard about that," I said.

"Oh, yeah? Did you see me on TV?"

"No. Bad reception."

Veronica sat beside me on the couch, kissed my cheek and told me I needed a shave. She pretended not to notice how banged up I looked. By this point in our relationship, she was over being surprised by my occasional scratches and bruises. I wanted to tell her what had happened. What I'd done. I was afraid of how she would take it, but I knew I could never keep something like that bottled up inside me for the rest of my life without telling someone, and it wasn't fair to continue seeing her without letting her know the kind of man she was with. I opened my mouth, but nothing came out.

"Poor kid," she said.

For a second, I thought she meant Samuel. She must have seen the shock on my face.

"What?" she asked. "What did I say?"

"You meant your nephew?"

"Yes, of course. My sister denies it, but I think he's a little slow. He can run and jump and climb like a monkey, but his brain can't quite keep up with his inquisitive nature."

"What's his name?" I asked.

"Sam," she said. When she said his name I feared my heart might quit in my chest, or skip so far out of beat that I'd collapse, but there wasn't a single flutter. I took a breath, slow and even. I let it out; did it over again. The earth abideth forever, and like that.

"Is the boy's name Sam Sloane?" I asked.

"No," she said, "my sister married a McGillicutty. *Sam Sloane*," she chided. "Did Sammy tell you I saw him yesterday?" I nodded. She explained how she'd wanted to go to Mrs. Sloane's funeral, but couldn't because of the drama with her nephew. I told her she hadn't missed much.

There was more small talk, more kissing, and then we moved to my bedroom and got undressed. She saw my bandages, touched them and cringed, not asking what had happened. Veronica was no one's fool. She knew a gun shot wound when she saw one, yet she was content to wait for my explanation.

I lay back on the bed and she straddled me. With my good hand I moved stray hair from her forehead, ran my fingers through its soft, auburn length. I worked my way down her throat, her shoulder, finally cupping her right breast. I moved my palm against her nipple and felt the rigid flesh tease my skin. With both of her hands free she definitely had the advantage. I asked if she'd like to travel, to get away from the neighborhood.

"For how long?" she asked.

"How does *forever* sound?"

"It sounds great," she said, "if you can last that long."

34 – *One tough librarian*

Later in the day, I drove Veronica home to collect her things—telling her to just pack enough for a few days, that we could pick up the rest of it later on, or buy anything else we might need. My most important items fit in a single suitcase, not counting the books—it would take a large truck to haul all of those. I'd try to come back for them once the situation settled down.

I didn't want to leave her alone, but I still had things to do. I started to hand her my .45—the good one with those shiny wear marks—but then I didn't think she'd ever use it, not even if her life depended on it. Instead, I snuck the weapon into her purse and told her to call me if she needed help.

"A lot of help I'm going to get from a man with his arm in a sling. Go on, get out of here. I'll be fine."

"You are one tough librarian," I said. "What do you do to those poor sods that bring in overdue books?"

"Just hope you never find out," she said.

The casual banter aside, she knew I meant it about calling, especially after I informed her not to tie up the line, "just in case."

"In case of *what*, Ben Franklin?"

"Complications," I said, scooting out the door before she could say more.

From her flat, down the stairs, and across the lot to where I'd parked my car, I felt damned near defenseless— one arm tied up, and no weapons on my person save for one fist, my feet, and my teeth. Before starting the engine, I reached under the seat to retrieve a snub-nosed revolver with recessed hammer. I never used it for jobs because the trigger had too light a pull. This was all I had in the vehicle, so it would have to do should I need it.

I made it back to my place without further incident, but I still had that niggling feeling of doom stirring the close-cropped hair at the nape of my neck. Someone was watching. I didn't know who, or from where, or for what purpose, but they were there all the same. Never before had I felt such thing—a black curtain of uncertainty hanging motionless, and seamless, in front of me. It seemed to be my destiny, to move toward it, to enter its inky folds, perhaps never to return.

I went inside my place and sat on the divan where I'd always liked to read while waiting for my next assignments. I stared at the neat rows of books, contemplating the off white paint, the cold sterility of it all— how fucking *empty* it felt, and how emblematic of my life without the one I loved with whom to share it. I was glad to leave it all behind—the place, the people, the work. To think that I'd wasted ten years of my life taking it away from others. The money had been good, but no amount of cash could justify what I'd done.

Shaking my head, I smiled, not about all those who had died by my hand, but at myself for philosophizing over a moot point. Nothing I could do about it now apart from accepting who I had been, and to believe that I could become someone better.

Samuel Sloane told me that I was a "good man." I was determined to prove him right. I got up to collect my things.

Just then someone knocked on the door.

35 – *No finesse*

The Swordsman stood in the open doorway, a lopsided grin making his face seem uneven, as if badly sculpted.

"You know why I've come," he said.

I stepped aside, showing him into the apartment. He moved around the living room, his hand in the air above the back of a chair, near a painting, a photo, poised, but never quite touching anything.

"How'd you kill Theo?" I asked.

"I see you're a man who appreciates stories." He indicated the books. I didn't answer, waiting for him to answer my question.

"I don't know, Mr. Franklin. Must have scared him to death," he said.

Very few knew my real name, but this guy had obviously been around long enough to know how to do the job—the one thing he and I both shared in common.

"That won't work on me," I said.

"Oh, really?" he asked, the odd grin returning as he spoke. "I'd have thought you'd be terrified that I might kidnap your tasty squeeze, and gut her like a fish."

Ah, well, I thought to myself, *one of the best assassins in the entire world, but his use of simile is a cliché.* Still, one can't have everything—except the truth was that he had *most* of it, and I'm sure he knew it.

"You'd have already killed her if that was your plan," I said.

"I might still do it, you know."

"And if you do, I'll come after you. *You know.*"

He flopped down on my couch, asked me to sit down so he didn't have to crane his neck to look up at me. I eased onto the divan where I'd been sitting when he knocked.

"You don't want to go up against me, Benjamin. You'll lose."

"I bet I'd give you a few uncomfortable nights before I do," I said.

This time, the grin broadened. Seeing so many teeth nudged the expression over into madness.

"Why'd you have to kill Theo?" I asked. "Who issued the contract?"

"I don't work for you," said the Swordsman, "and I certainly never kiss and tell. Suffice to say that the old man had something that didn't belong to him. I was sent to reclaim it. I sliced up Laurel and Hardy as a means of letting him know the score, but he chose to ignore the message. I admired his fortitude, but let's face it—his behavior was rude."

"And what if the boss hadn't known—had, in fact, no foreknowledge with which to comprehend your signal?"

The Swordsman turned his head to one side, contemplating, seeming to add up certain facts in his brain, until that bizarre smile returned.

"Come to think of it, I guess he really didn't know, did he? But *you* do!"

And like that, I knew what he was after.

"One of the other families hired you to get back their drugs?" I laughed.

"That's a lot of product, my friend. Only an idiot would try to fuck over my client and think he could get away with it. Did you believe you could? You're just an ex-soldier who used to be a decent shot."

"Decent enough to kill Fincino, and most of the shit-for-brains assholes he employed. And I did them all in one night," I said. "Not that I'm bragging. Truth is that I'm done with that life."

The Swordsman looked pained. "Give up all of this?" he asked, his hand moving around in an arc delineating not the space of my living room, but the great wide world beyond. "This entire planet is a killing ground; you can't escape it. Face it, my friend; it's what you do."

"*Did* is the operative verb, and I'm not your friend. You want the meth, you're welcome to it. Come with me."

I rose, but had barely cleared my ass from the chair when he was up, across the room, and on me—twelve inches of cold steel at my throat.

"You fool," he said. "I already told you I don't take orders from you."

"I've had about enough of this bullshit. Slit my throat, if you're going to, otherwise, take whatever you came for and get the fuck out of my life."

The Swordsman had me in a half-Nelson, holding the sore side, of course. I sucked in a quick breath, the soreness of the wound an excruciating inferno. He held the long knife out in front of my face, moving it just right until we could see the reflection of our eyes in the polished steel. I remember his were mismatched, one hazel, the other dark brown. The tip of the blade touched my ear, my cheek, and moved close to my left eye. For whatever reason, I couldn't blink.

Infuriated that I was beyond intimidation, he pushed me down onto the carpet, stepped on my back and said "Your beloved boss took the coward's way out. I found a bottle of pills and a fifth of Jack Daniels on the table when I entered his office. Both were empty."

"You lie," I said, and for the first time since he'd entered the apartment, I was truly pissed.

The Swordsman laughed.

"Such emotion! And from one who was never known to express it. What changed, Benjamin? Did killing your partner…"

I rolled, driving my good arm up into his groin. He tried to leap away from me, but he wasn't fast enough. He sprawled, one hand nursing his aching balls, but he still held the blade in the other. I got to my feet, tore the automatic from my pocket and pointed it at his right eye—the hazel one.

"What is it with you ramrods and guns? Absolutely no finesse," he said. "If you only understood the way things stand."

"I understand more than I want to," I said. "I know that you figured out a way to kill Papa Theo so it looked like suicide, and that you did so because you and your client thought he'd screwed them out of Fincino's drugs. The problem is that you wasted your time and effort because Theo didn't ask me to whack Jimmy Finch, or to take his stash of meth. I did all of that on my own, as recompense for the life of a guy I hardly even knew. I didn't even know about the fucking drugs until I opened the bag the next day. I meant to tell the boss about them, but got sidetracked with other things. After all the shit's that happened this week, I figured Theo'd had more than his share of sorrows, and that I'd find a way to deal with this on my own."

"Well," he whispered, getting his breath back. "One way or another, I guess you're about to do so."

I wanted to kill this asshole. The desire to do so welled up in me stronger than any emotion I'd ever felt in my entire life, yet… *Yet*, I thought. *Killing him will mean the situation continues; someone else will come looking, and another, and another, ad infinitum, world without end.*

"I told you, I'm done with killing," I said, "unless you make me do it. Now, do you want the dope or not?"

The Swordsman nodded.

I told him to sheath the blade and to precede me down the stairs. I pointed out which car was mine, but it was obvious he already knew. After popping the trunk, I motioned for him to take the bag. Lying next to it was the briefcase full of bonds.

"What's in the case?" he asked.

"A Desert Eagle," I said. "Just a backup piece I sometime use. You want it? You can have that too."

"Guns," he said, no attempt to hide his disgust.

"It's a .50 caliber—top of the line," I said. "Blow a hole in a guy the size of a melon."

"That takes all the fun out of it," he said. "I like working with my hands, and am not afraid of getting them dirty."

The Swordsman took the duffle bag, showed me that lopsided grin again, and walked away.

"We're done," I said.

"For now," he replied.

"I mean it. I don't want to see you again."

"Oh, you can trust to that, Benjamin. If there's a next time, and I so hope that there will be, you certainly won't see me coming. Not until I'm close enough to cut out your heart."

"What's the percentage in killing a low-level enforcer like me?" I asked.

The man looked chagrined, as if I'd asked why two-plus-two equaled four.

"I don't need the money, Benjamin. I do this because I *like* it."

I watched him walk away, get into what looked like a European sports car, and drive away. He didn't look back, but I felt his eyes on me just the same.

I climbed the stairs feeling so used up there seemed virtually nothing left. I noticed the bloodstained coat I'd had on the day before, lying over the back of a kitchen chair and remembered the envelope D'Amato had given me. It was still there, unopened, in the breast pocket. I fished it out to examine it more closely. Between two of my own bloody fingerprints was my name—*Benjamin*—written in Theo's own delicate hand.

The thing was stuffed with cash. Holding it in my good hand, I used my teeth to tear off an end and dumped out the contents. Inside were a thousand one-hundred dollar bills, two photographs, and a note from Papa Theo. In the latter, he acknowledged how proud he was of me, how happy he'd been with my "progress" throughout the years. He wrote of how he used to pray for a son to continue after he had "retired," but how Fate had thrown him a curve. At first I thought maybe he was talking about *me* since there was obviously no way the organization would allow someone like myself to step into his shoes—not only because I wasn't genuine family, I wasn't *family* in any sense—not even Italian. The Franklins had come over from Great Britain, but through my father's work for Papa Theo and others, I'd been accepted into the culture—a *paisan* by proxy.

I read the rest of the note and realized that the boss hadn't meant me. The last paragraph clued me to the truth— revealing a secret that, for all my seeming powers of observation, I'd never suspected until the very end.

I read through the letter twice more then set it aside. I picked up the photos, the first one very old and mounted on a thick piece of cardstock. The paper was brown with age. It showed a chubby-faced rascal wearing old-fashioned knickers. The kid had on a dark beret, cocked at a jaunty angle atop a head full of curly locks. In a bit of space near the bottom of the image were the words *Theodore ha quattro anni* written in an elegant script. The other was a more modern snapshot of another little boy sitting on a swing. This one wore a dreamy expression on his mug, but had the saddest eyes you ever saw on a child. On the back of the image someone had scribbled lightly in pencil, *Samuel Sloane – age six*.

I took the photos over to the window and held them up to the light. Papa Theo and Sammy. Two kids from two different worlds, yet it was plain for anyone to see that, at this young age, they looked exactly the same.

I scooped up the thick pile of bills, stuck them in another envelope and printed "Please Pray for Samuel Sloane" on the back flap. On my way to pick up Veronica, I stopped by the church and slid the cash into the alms box as I'd done with the bills I'd taken from the banker. It was a lot of dough, but it didn't belong to me. I'd earned enough blood money already—no way I would profit from the death of my only friend.

Soon after, I had Veronica in the car and was about to pull away from the curb to begin our journey. Instead, I shifted into neutral and sat there idling.

"Did we forget something?"

"You didn't," I told her, "but I did."

She gave me a funny look. Awkward as it was I knew I had to tell her, at least some of it, before we drove away. After hearing what I had to say she might feel differently about me. She needed to understand the facts in order to make an informed decision.

"What is it?"

I asked if she knew who I worked for and she nodded. The way her eyes sort of glazed over let me know she didn't approve. I then asked if she knew exactly what I did for the organization. She shook her head, looked down into her lap then back at me.

"Benjamin," she said, a nervous smile making delicate lines appear around her mouth, "you're not going to talk me out of loving you."

"I just—"

"You're a good man, my love. That's all that matters."

I sat there for another minute, thinking about her words, thinking *if you only knew*. I would find a way to tell her, and sooner than later. In the meantime, I put the autoMobile in gear and we headed north out of the city. As we were getting onto the highway a tractor-trailer's horn blared forth like a trumpet of doom, the driver nearly running us off the road.

"What an asshole!" V said. "Damn! If only I had a gun!"

I looked at her handbag on the seat between us and laughed. When she asked me what was so funny, I just shook my head and laughed some more. I laughed so hard I came close to tearing out my stitches. *Laughing like that could kill a man*, I thought, but I knew from experience there are far worse ways to go.

FIN

ABOUT THE AUTHOR:

G. Warlock Vance established himself first as a writer of horror fiction before moving on to mystery and suspense. His influences range from Paul Auster to Carlos Ruiz Zafón, with various eras of writing and genres in between. Warlock is first to admit that his latest novel, THE BAD MAN, owes a debt to authors Raymond Chandler and Dashiell Hammett, with a wee dash of Stieg Larsson tossed in for added spice.

In addition to his fiction writing, Warlock is a professor of English Literature. He teaches at a small college in North Carolina.

CPSIA information can be obtained
at www.ICGtesting.com
Printed in the USA
FFOW03n1724121115
18394FF